I0699708

GREENBUTTON

KAYLA GARNETT COOK

Published by Kayla Garnett Cook
Copyright © 2022 Kayla Garnett Cook
GreenButton
All rights reserved. No part of this book can be reproduced or used in any manner unless it's a brief quote for a book review.
Contact: info@kaylagarnettcook.com

Printed Worldwide
First Edition 2022
First Printing 2022

ISBN (PB): 979-8-9854423-0-4
ISBN (HB): 979-8-9854423-1-1
ISBN (eBook): 979-8-9854423-2-8
LCCN: 2021924948

Kayla Garnett Cook
PO Box 254
Berwick, Iowa 50032
kaylagarnettcook.com

To anyone who has ever held back a tear . . .

1

AUSTIN

"I just *love* these Q&A things." Riley pursed his lips, glaring at the stage as we stood in the wing. "I mean, why don't we just add a Frequently Asked Questions section on our website?" Riley gasped. "Oh, wait . . . !" His eyes widened as he shook his head slightly. "We already have one!"

Sam looked up at him through his beady dark brown eyes, ignoring Riley's remark. I chose not to comment, stuffing my hand in my pocket to pull out my phone and see if Cara, my wife, had responded. I pressed the green home button sticker, but no notifications appeared—only my wallpaper of Cara holding Kaleigha and Bella, our baby girls, chilling on the couch in our living room.

Tennyson folded his arms, sighing, looking at us as if this would be the most tedious task he had ever done.

"You don't have to go," Chris said to Riley, his older brother.

"Nate would fire me from the band," Riley told him.

"We've already tried to fire you." I smirked, nudging his arm.

"And I've tried to leave," Riley shot back.

"I mean, bass players are replaceable." Chris's face twitched.

"Someone's gotta keep y'all on your toes." Riley widened his hazel eyes before narrowing them.

"Riley," Tennyson didn't skip a beat, "three of us already have kids. We don't need another."

"You want me, though!" Riley's lips curled in the corners.

"Only because it's too much work to find someone else." Chris ruffled his brother's wavy reddish-brown hair.

Forcefully removing his little brother's hand from his head by grabbing Chris's wrist, Riley shoved him into the blue concrete wall. "Chris, I got you into this band, and I can get you out of it."

Without warning, Chris jumped on Riley's back, covering Riley's eyes with his hands.

"Chris! I swear to God . . . !" Riley backed up into Tennyson.

"Guys!" Tennyson yelled, pushing Riley's arm. "Y'all are grown men, acting like frickin' middle schoolers. Grow up!"

Through my embarrassed laughter, I exclaimed, "Y'all are so dramatic!" Murmurs of small talk sounded out from the worship center. We were about to lose fans before the show even started.

Riley forced Chris's arms off of his neck, digging his nails into his brother's hand in the process as Chris yelped, "Ow!" Chris wrapped his legs around Riley's waist, managing to embrace Riley again.

Nate, our manager, burst through the door. "Hey. People can hear you." His voice sounded stern. "You need to be out there . . ." He pulled out his brand-new smartphone. ". . . T-minus two minutes ago, so y'all need to go."

Riley tore Chris's legs off of him as if he was ripping off a seat belt on an airplane.

I checked my phone one more time. My messages to Cara showed "Delivered." I had already rebooted my phone, so it wasn't a connection issue. Why wasn't Cara answering? Maybe she was napping because she hadn't been feeling well over the last few days. I shouldn't have left her.

As my chest tightened, Tennyson proceeded to stage right, and the pissed-off Riley followed him onto the stage. I followed Riley.

This sanctuary was wide open. So many churches we had visited lacked windows, which made their worship centers dark and compacted. Not this church. The chairs shone a bright blue, and the windows were bare, not blanketed by shades that would close worship off to the outside world.

The guys and I sat on stools. Only Sam and I sat between Riley and Chris. Their quarrel had gone a little too far, even for them. There were probably forty or fifty people in the sanctuary. Everyone at this point was VIP and here for the Q&A, all sitting in the middle section of the first five rows.

Clasping my hands together, I looked around for an available mic, but George, our sound guy, wasn't in the sound booth. I decided it would be easier if we just raised our voices. "All right," I said, "so we're GreenButton, and my name is Austin Brooklyn. I'm the voice you hear on the radio when you hear a GreenButton song, so if you don't like my voice, I'm sorry." I put a hand up. "But the good news is there's a bit of guitar, bass, piano, and drums that these guys play to make everything sound good." I glanced over at

Sam and Chris, then Riley and Tennyson. "Sam, do you wanna start by introducing yourself and what you play?"

"My name is Sam Lowe," Sam's voice boomed, confident but calm. "I play keys."

Both Riley and Chris attempted to introduce themselves in the same millisecond.

"You can go," Riley told his brother, leaning in to see past Sam and me.

"No, no, you go," Chris countered.

Riley smirked with a mischievous look in his eyes. "No, no, *no*, little bro, *you* go."

"So, yeah, that's Riley," Chris announced. "Riley Thompson claims to be my older brother because we were raised by the same people and have the same last name, but I'm pretty sure I'm adopted, or maybe I was switched at birth because I'm nothing like my family." This was very true. Chris was the white sheep of the Thompson family. A down-to-earth guy, his blond hair capped off his small, skinny frame. Their dad, a burly tattoo artist, was probably in a motorcycle gang. Their mom wore too much makeup, and she'd enveloped her arms in tattoos. Riley, too, was inked everywhere. Chris was not. The Thompsons, minus Chris, were tough-looking people and rough around the edges. My mother had even discouraged me from hanging around them because she was pretty sure they smoked weed. But the Thompsons loved Jesus and could smoke a real mean pork chop.

"What's your name again?" Riley asked sarcastically.

"Christopher." Chris scanned the audience. "See, he doesn't even know who I am."

"So, what do y'all do in the band?" Sam pretended to wonder aloud.

"Riley doesn't do anything," Chris didn't skip a beat.

"Well, I at least pretend to play bass," Riley scoffed.

The crowd laughed awkwardly.

"I *actually* play guitar," Chris snickered.

"So, anyway," Tennyson cut them off, "I'm Tennyson Peterson. I got on the wrong bus, don't know these guys, but since I'm here, I guess I'll play some drums."

"What a servant heart," I said. Then I realized we forgot to pray. "We should probably pray before diving into this Q&A, and then we'll get started." I bowed my head. "Hey, God . . ." I took a deep breath, trying to regroup myself for the moment. "I just want to thank You for bringing us to Hartford where we have the opportunity to meet some really incredible people here tonight. I wanna thank You for the hospitality of this church and for everyone sitting in this room. Tonight, I ask that You give every single person who walks through these doors peace in knowing the Truth of who You are. I ask that You let the Truth of the cross overwhelm the hearts in this room. Let any walls be broken down that need to be broken down in order to see what Your grace and peace is. Yeah, God, we love You a lot. All these things, in Jesus's name, amen."

As soon as I said amen, I wondered if I had forgotten anything. There was always so much pressure in praying out loud.

My eyes adjusted to the light again. "Okay, so we have time for a few questions, and if we don't get to yours, it's not personal, I promise. Just raise your hand, and we'll call on you."

I called on the first hand I saw, a young girl who was maybe twelve or so. "Yes, ma'am, in the blue shirt, here, up front. What's your name?"

Her grin revealed a mouth full of shiny metal braces. "Lauren."

"Hey, Lauren," I said in my customer service voice.

She rubbed her hands together and asked, "What's the funniest thing that has ever happened during a concert?"

I smirked. Riley kept his eyes straight ahead while Sam raised his eyebrows, waiting to see if I would talk.

"So," I said, "one time, I was singing, ya know, because that's what I do apparently, and it was a festival—" I started laughing. "—okay, I can't do this."

"Oh, my gosh," Sam muttered, rolling his eyes. He had heard me tell this story a hundred times.

I pinched my index finger and my thumb together, zipping the air down, trying to compose myself. "And it was outside." I couldn't help but laugh through this. "I was on the part of the stage that goes out into the audience—the part shaped like a 'T'—and the mic that I'd been holding flew out of my hands, probably because my hands were sweating from the humidity. And the band didn't know what had happened, so they, of course, kept playing while I crawled around the stage looking for the mic. I think eventually I was on my knees, reaching my hands out, hoping for the mic to be returned, but people thought I was high fiving them or having a Holy Spirit moment or whatever. And this went on for the better part of the song. Luckily, Nate, our manager, ran onto the stage with an extra mic and saved the day, as always. Shout out to Nate! And to this day, we aren't sure where that microphone went." I cleared my throat, trying to sound serious. "So, if anyone has information about the stolen microphone in Kansas, please email our management, because those things are expensive." I paused. "Also, that's why we don't have mics for this Q&A." There were a few chuckles from the audience. I heard a few women laugh out loud, but I couldn't place who had laughed.

"Actually," Chris said, "Riley just didn't do his job." That had never been Riley's job.

"Oh, yeah." Riley folded his arms. "It's always the older sibling's fault. Can I get a round of applause for older sibling awareness?"

For the small number of people in the room, that comment garnered a lot of acknowledgment through cheers and claps—and even a few "whoots!"

"Okay . . ." I thought about my own older brothers, and I was ready to move on. "Next question . . . goes to . . ." I saw a cute blonde girl in a tight leather jacket. "Gal in the middle, wearing black." I wondered if she was single, despite the jacked bald guy next to her. *What is wrong with me?*

"What's the story behind 'Let Me Trust You'?"

Sam and I exchanged glances. I braced myself, unsure of how to say what I was about to say without it hitting too close to home. I just had to go for it. "I wrote that song at like two in the morning of—I guess the morning after the Sandy Hook shootings." I put my hands up. "And I'm sorry to bring it up, especially because I know this is close to home for a lot of you." I took in a deep breath, shaking my head, my face radiating heat. "We had considered canceling the show that day because we were doing a Christmas show in Buffalo, and it just didn't feel right to celebrate when there was so much pain in the nation. When I asked my wife, Cara, if we should do the show that afternoon, she reminded me that a Christmas show was probably what people needed. They needed the hope of the cross. I remember telling her I was sad, even as an outsider looking in, and then she told me that maybe the message isn't to shove Jesus down people's throats in the midst of pain but to pray for faith in the times of loss."

I sighed, looking back at the chick who'd asked the question, hating that I'd just brought that up to a room full of people who might've been personally affected by that. I stared down for a second as I heard someone sniff. Hopefully, they just had allergies. "I realized that trusting God—while it's a choice—is also a gift, and sometimes all you can do is ask Him for help in trusting Him, especially during the moments where you just don't feel it and you don't know why. However, it doesn't matter if you have a mustard seed of faith or a tree of faith—God's love for you does not change."

Within the silence that followed, I remembered I still had to call on someone. "Um, next question . . . !" There was some awkward enthusiasm in my voice as I scanned the seats. A lady, probably about my mom's age, raised her hand. She stood near the back with her two daughters. "Yes, ma'am—" My voice caught in between saying *ma'am* and *mom.* "—in the red, in the back."

"Austin, what's the story behind the mint green earring?"

Running my finger over the square resin earring, I twisted it. "Okay, so yeah, it's kind of a weird story because there was a lady in Oregon a few years ago who told me that the Holy Spirit wanted her to give me these earrings after a show. Now, why she had an extra pair of earrings on her person that night? I have no idea. She told me we were supposed to split up the band once they both fell out. Riley even pierced my ears that night. The people at Walmart didn't question why we were buying needles at 1:00 a.m. One of them fell out within a few weeks. Anyway, I'm not really sure it's Biblical, but hey, the Lord works in mysterious ways, and I feel like if God wants to work through earrings that some lady gave me, then I'm not gonna put it past Him. So far, though, I don't see a reason to split up the band."

I called on the next hand I saw. It belonged to a plump lady, sitting in the back. She appeared to be alone.

Unable to hear what she asked at first, I asked her to speak up a bit.

"How did you get the name GreenButton?" she repeated.

"Oh, that's a great question." A question that was indeed answered on the FAQ section on our website. Pulling my lips into my mouth, I decided to let one of the other guys chime in because I was talking too much.

"Before Sam," Chris said, placing a hand on Sam's shoulder for a moment, "we had Keaton, who quit the band to pursue a pastoral calling. He played piano for us, and our band needed a name for a Christmas Eve service flyer. We were gonna be featured, which was a super big deal for us, especially given the size of our growing church. We threw around names, and then finally Keaton suggested 'green button.' And we were like, 'no.' Then he asked us if we had any better ideas, but we didn't. Apparently, Keaton's little sister really wanted an MP3 player with a green button, because she was obsessed with the color green."

"We send her a royalty for everything we do," I added. When the laughter from the audience faded out, I said, "I'm just kidding, but maybe we should."

"Yeah, maybe we should," Chris agreed. "I mean, we always talked about changing it, but then our merchandise had green buttons on it. And then we started putting little green button stickers on the home buttons of our phones. And then we started selling those. And then we were too far into it to stop."

"One more question," Nate called, cupping his mouth with one hand, from the side wing of the backstage.

"The boss says we have time for one more," I announced, "so it better be a good one."

A dude in the middle of several girls near the front raised his hand. Probably in college or so, he wore a black T-shirt with our button on it.

"My man, wearing the GreenButton shirt, what's up?"

"How did each of you get into the band?"

"When I was fourteen," Tennyson said, "I was grounded, per usual, and my mom found an ad in the paper, seeking a drummer for a church band, and she told me that could be my alternate punishment." He paused. "But it worked out because I started going to youth group where I met Jesus. Even though Austin, Keaton, Chris, and Riley were already best friends, they really welcomed me right away when they didn't have to."

"Awww." Riley pretended to wipe a tear from his eye.

"Your mom actually pays us," I told him. "You're still being punished."

"Still?" Tennyson asked.

"Yeah, you didn't know?" Riley didn't give Tennyson a chance to respond. "I joined the band during my sophomore year because they needed a bass player, and then Chris insisted on joining, too, because he thought he could play guitar."

"I learned how to play acoustic guitar when I was ten," Chris added, "and Riley wanted to be cool, but acoustic was too hard for him. I was only thirteen when I joined the youth worship team, which eventually became the band."

"Sam." I placed a hand on his shoulder. "How'd you get here?"

"Uh, well, I learned how to play the piano during my freshman year of high school, and then I started writing music, doing covers, and some of my own stuff on YouTube. I also shared my testimony about why I started pursuing music and faith, which sort of went viral before going viral was cool. I went to GreenButton's home church in high school, and I knew who they were—didn't realize they knew who *I* was, even though I was on the worship team and would see them in passing when they would come back for visits. And then one day Austin came up to me in the spring of my senior year, and I almost passed out when he knew my name—but he asked me to hop on the bus with them after I graduated high school to play the piano. I was only seventeen, so basically, I was kidnapped."

Even though part of me wanted Sam to dive deeper into his testimony, I understood why he didn't throw it around; his parents were killed in a car wreck when he was thirteen.

"Yeah, maybe don't tell that to the whole world," I joked. "We don't want to get thrown in jail."

"Why not? That could be your testimony," Sam told me.

"No, that's gonna be Riley's testimony," Chris countered, and his tone made me wonder if Chris was surprised Riley wasn't in jail. Sometimes I was surprised Riley wasn't in jail . . .

"Yeah, we'll cross that bridge when we come to it." I didn't want this conversation to sound like we were condemning or downgrading felons. We had all been dealt different cards. Then I realized I hadn't answered the question. "I guess for me, I didn't realize we were even a band until we needed a name, because I thought we were just the student ministry worship band. And I thought the guys were just humoring me by letting me play some of the songs I had written."

"Tennyson's mom was paying us for you, too," Riley told me.

Chuckling, I rolled my eyes. "Let's pray out."

2

AUSTIN

I noticed my phone buzzing on the table when we got to the room where our stuff was, and it was Charlie, Cara's dad. My heart dropped. *Please let this be a butt dial.*

"Hey, what's up?" I answered.

"Austin," he said, "I have some really bad news."

"What? Is everyone okay?" I started to walk out of the room, even though I really wanted the food.

"Um, no." He cleared his throat. "Cara passed away this afternoon." His voice rocked.

"Wait. What?" I must've heard him wrong. That was impossible, I thought to myself, taking in the blue concrete wall as it closed in on me, swallowing me whole.

"You know how she wasn't feeling well—the paramedic said it may have been an infection from the mission trip."

"So, she's like *gone*, gone?"

"Yeah, she is dead." There was a disconnect in his voice.

"Are you sure?" I traced my hand over the grain of the blue on the wall.

"Donna and I went to the house to check on her because she wasn't responding to her messages all afternoon, and we were going to come anyway to take care of the girls, so she could rest, and then we came in and she was—she didn't have a pulse. Kaleigha was upstairs crying in her crib. We called 9-1-1, tried CPR, but she was—she was gone." His voice cracked at the end.

My body hollowed. My vision blurred. My face burned from the inside out.

"I . . ." Opening my mouth, I choked on my words. I wondered if things would've been different had I been there. "Are the girls okay?" I barely recognized my own voice as it shook.

"Yeah, they're . . . they're okay."

"Do they—does Kaleigha know what happened?"

"The paramedic explained it to her."

"What did she say?"

"She cried, not really understanding, still wanting Cara." His voice broke.

Unable to speak, feeling my chin tremble, I steadied it with my free hand, wondering how people held back tears because I could not. The thought of Kaleigha calling out for Cara. No response because her mother was dead. Knowing that my kids felt alone and scared and neglected . . .

"Are you okay?" he asked after a moment.

My hand covered my mouth and nose, catching warm tears as I somehow managed to say, "I don't even know what to do."

"Yeah, that's understandable. Um, do you want to tell your manager and try to get back to Nashville?"

I wiped my nose as Chris walked by. I avoided eye contact with him. "Yeah, does Kelly know?"

"No, I'm calling her next."

"Who should I tell?"

"Um, tell who you need to tell. I mean, it's up to you, but I'd prefer you don't make it public until we get a chance to tell all of our close friends and family."

"Okay, thanks, Charlie."

"Thank you. Keep us updated on when you're going to be back and if you can get a flight out."

"I will. Bye."

"Bye, kiddo."

I hung up. Cara and the girls, my wallpaper, stared back at me. Locking the phone, turning the screen black, I stared down at the green button for a second. A tear splashed onto it, so I wiped my phone against my jeans before sliding it into my pocket. Rubbing my eyes with my palms, I felt a hand on my back. I didn't flinch.

"Are you okay?" I heard Chris's voice.

Shaking my head, I couldn't even look at him. "Where's Nate?"

"I don't know. What's wrong?" he asked quickly.

"You know how Cara wasn't feeling well?"

Chris nodded.

"She—she—her parents found her, and—Chris, she's . . . She—they think it was an infection from the mission trip or something, but she . . ." My voice broke. "She's with Jesus."

3

CHRIS

When he said those words, everything around me went silent, including him. The air grew thinner. The colors of the hallway grayed and dimmed.

"No," I murmured.

He kept his eyes on the floor when I stole a glance his way.

"Man, I'm so sorry." I pulled him close, not sure if he'd push me away, but he returned the embrace. I felt him shake.

He let out a sob, and I asked quietly, keeping a grip on his shoulder, "What can I do?"

Burying his face in his hands, wiping his face, he said, "I don't know. Go find Nate." He looked up at me, his blue eyes vivid with tears and red blood vessels.

"I'll call him." I pulled out my phone, realizing it would be on me to tell Megan, my wife, Cara's best friend, about this.

Nate didn't answer. "I'll go find him." I squeezed his shoulder before walking away in the opposite direction of the room the other guys were in. "You want me to tell him?"

"Yeah."

Figuring that Nate was probably running around, busy with managerial duties, I decided to check the merch table. Speed walking, I ran into him on the way there.

"Hey, can we chat?"

"Not right now." He walked past me.

"Nate, it's an emergency," I told him, turning around to follow him.

He stopped walking, folding his arms. "What, Chris?"

We stood alone in the hallway. "Cara passed away."

No longer annoyed, he stepped back, stuffing his hands into his pockets. "Cara? Cara Brooklyn?" He didn't believe me.

"Yes. They think she had an infection from the mission trip she went on. Austin just told me. He's looking for you."

Keeping his gaze straight ahead, he whispered, "Wow." Then he mumbled, "This is above my paygrade." He looked back at me. "Where is he?"

"Just down the hall. Come on."

We found Austin sitting against the wall, on his phone. He looked up. "Hey. Did Chris tell you?"

Nate nodded as he sat next to him. "Yeah."

I sat on the other side of Austin, using my knees as an armrest.

"What do you want to do?" Nate asked him.

"Fly out tonight if we can."

"I assume you're not going to do the show."

"Yeah, no." Austin pinched his nose.

"Okay." Nate looked at me. "Can you guys start looking at plane tickets? Logan is probably the closest airport that would get you back to Nashville. I'll let the Resin Ring crew know, and then they can decide what they want to do."

I stepped outside to tell Megan.

When she answered the phone, she said, "Hey, what's up?"

Pacing on the wet pavement, I didn't even know where to begin. "Um . . ." How was I supposed to tell her that her best friend was dead? I stared at people walking by, hoping they wouldn't stop and try to chat. "I don't know a good way to say this, but Cara passed away."

"What?"

I swallowed, unable to speak.

"I literally just talked to her this morning," she continued.

"What time?" Maybe something was miscommunicated. Maybe Cara was fine.

"Around 10:30. Chris, she was—she said she had a temp of 102, and I told her she needed to go to the doctor, but she said that was too much work, and she wanted to just sleep." Then she paused. "I should've told her to go to the hospital," she cried.

"Megan. No."

"Chris, I should've—"

"No, Megan, you didn't know. Who would've thought?"

"She's actually gone?" she asked quietly.

"Yeah. I'm sorry." My eyes burned with hot water as I heard a sob come through my words.

"How's Austin?"

"Not great." I gasped for air. "We're going to try to fly back to Nashville tonight, but I'll keep you updated."

"Okay." I could tell if she wasn't already crying, she was about to. "Are you coming with him?"

"That's my hope, because I know this is difficult, to say the least, and I don't want Austin to fly back alone. But he gets priority if there's only one ticket."

"Makes sense. How are you doing, Chris?" Her voice tightened.

"I . . ." It was sweet that she took the time to ask. "It doesn't really seem real, and I'm worried about how it's going to affect everything."

"Yeah," she agreed. "Does Elena know?" Elena was Tennyson's wife.

"Um, I think Tennyson's gonna tell Elena."

"Should I tell anyone?"

"Uhhh . . ." I leaned against the stone exterior of the church. "I honestly don't know. I'll get back to you on that. I just found out, too."

"Okay."

"But I'll keep you updated. And I'll call you when I know whether we're gonna fly out."

"Okay. Thank you."

"Thank you. Hang in there. I love you."

There was a 9:00 p.m. flight out of Boston, and there were two seats open. We ordered plane tickets from Nate's phone with Austin's credit card and printed the tickets off at the church. A staff member of the church was kind enough to drive us to Logan from Hartford. Austin was usually outgoing to a fault, even when things weren't going perfectly, but he barely said anything the whole ride there, so I didn't say much either. Hopefully, the lady understood we weren't being rude.

When we got to the airport, we didn't even have time to grab a snack, because we wanted to double check we'd be able to board before our driver left. By the grace of God, everything went through.

Austin remained silent through most of the flight. I asked the stewardess for a snack, but after a few bites of the stale mini pretzels, I lost my appetite.

When we got off the plane, Austin called Cara's dad, Charlie, to track him down. Austin and I only had backpacks on us. I scooted in the back of the overpriced truck, letting Austin take the front.

"I'm so sorry," I told Charlie quietly, placing a light touch on his shoulder from the back, misting up as I said it.

"Thanks, Chris." Charlie looked at Austin, putting the truck in drive. "How are you, kiddo?"

"I'm . . ." Austin stared straight ahead. "I'm okay. I just wish I had been home."

Charlie grabbed Austin by the wrist of his black silk jacket. "We all do."

Silence.

"Would things have been different if she would've gotten to the hospital?" Austin worked up the courage to ask.

"There's no way to know, kiddo."

"I shouldn't have left her home sick." The pain conquered his voice.

"I'm not going to even let you entertain that idea, buddy; it's nobody's fault. Things happen."

I thought about Megan.

"Cara would not let you think that even for a second," I reminded him.

"No, she wouldn't," Charlie agreed.

Austin focused his gaze on the rear of the vehicle in front of us.

"You hear me?" If someone didn't speak English, they'd think Charlie was mad at Austin because of his tone.

"Yeah." Austin's mind was still in Connecticut.

4

RILEY

"I have an idea," Kelly, my girlfriend, announced. I sat next to her, and Austin was still at the table next to Donna, Kelly and Cara's mother.

"What?" I asked her.

Kelly turned sideways on the couch to look at Austin. "What if we started a GoFundMe, so y'all could have a bit of time off and not have to worry about the label?"

Austin and I exchanged glances as he ran a hand through his hair, staring at her.

"I don't wanna ask people for money," he told her.

"Yeah, but then you can be home for a while—at least for a few weeks, because you're losing money by the second from canceling shows and stuff."

"True."

"You don't need another thing to worry about right now." Donna patted Austin on the shoulder before walking into the living room.

Austin clasped his hands together, looking down.

"I could start a GoFundMe for you guys," Kelly told him.

"What about you?" Austin asked her.

"Eh, I'll be okay. I'm doing Friday night's show."

"I don't even know how I can go back on tour." Austin voiced what we were all thinking.

"Yeah, who'd watch your kids?" I asked.

"We could." Donna had told Austin this earlier in the afternoon, too.

"For the rest of the tour?" he asked.

"Yeah. Charlie and I would support you in every way possible. If that means you want to continue to tour, we'll take care of the girls. If it means you wanna stay home for a little while, we'll support you that way, too. We're all in this together. It's what Cara would want."

"Thank you," Austin said quietly. "That means a lot. And the same goes for you guys, Donna."

"Same here," Kelly told Austin.

"I third that," I told him.

Austin swallowed hard. "Thank you."

"I'm going to start the GoFundMe," Kelly told him, "because being on the road is the last thing you need to worry about right now."

"Only if you take half for you and your crew," Austin told her.

"We don't have kids, and we're only missing tonight's show. We're fine."

"Do you think we'll ever get to go back on tour?" I asked Austin.

Austin shrugged before leaning back in the wooden chair, gripping the back of his neck.

"He probably doesn't know right now," Donna scolded me.

"Yeah, I'm not really sure what to do," he agreed.

"I'm gonna start the GoFundMe." Kelly looked at me. "You're responsible for putting it on the band's social media accounts, okay?"

"I can do that." Then I looked at Austin. "I think Chris announced what happened on social media, right?"

Austin nodded. "Yeah, he did."

"It was really well written," Kelly said.

"Yeah, I didn't read it," Austin stated, leaning back in the chair again.

"When are your parents coming?" Kelly asked him.

"Tonight."

"And they're staying with you?"

"Yup."

Kelly grabbed her laptop from the coffee table and sauntered over to the table to sit next to him. Joining them, I let Kelly open the GoFundMe account on her own. She didn't need my help.

* * *

As the family finalized the funeral plans, Kelly gasped curse words.

"What?" All day, Austin had been quiet. Tired. Sad.

"What?" Donna asked her.

Kelly showed Austin her phone, and Donna looked over his shoulder, saying, "Wow! They really like you." She squeezed his shoulder.

Austin looked back up at Kelly in awe. "Is this accurate?" His voice cracked.

"It is."

"We hit the goal already?" He took the phone from her, checking it out himself.

"We did."

Still at the table he hadn't left since I'd gotten here, I could see his eyes welling up. He grabbed his cheeks, blinking several times.

"Are you okay?" Kelly asked, plopping down next to him on the chair.

He shrugged, biting his trembling lip, and I looked away. Even if it was a response to something really beautiful, it didn't change the fact that Cara was gone.

5

AUSTIN

I handed Bella, my younger one, off to Kelly before heading into our worship center with my mom by my side. The lights were dim as I held Kaleigha, my older one, on my hip. My wife's body lay in the casket. Her curly blonde hair turned into a blur of sand. I shifted Kaleigha as she started to slip from my hip. I would never look into Cara's aquamarine eyes again on this side of Heaven. I took in a deep breath, shifting Kaleigha, who pointed. "Mommy."

Donna and Charlie had already explained to Kaleigha what had happened. Kaleigha kind of understood that Cara's body didn't work on Earth, but there was a place where people went after their body didn't work that our eyes couldn't see. "Me want Mommy."

"I know." My throat closed in, and I could hear the pain in my own voice. Mom rubbed my back.

"Won't wake up?" Kaleigha's small voice filled my ears as well as my eyes.

Shaking my head, I kissed her hair as she laid her cheek against my chest, staring at her mommy.

She shrieked, "Me want 'er, Daddy!"

"*Shhh—shhh,*" I whispered, gazing up at the engineering of the lights and ceiling, holding her even tighter.

Unable to even look at the wax figure of Cara sleeping in her pastel pink dress, Mom wrapped an arm around me.

"Wake Mommy up," Kaleigha tried to reason.

My chin quivered as I pulled my lips into my mouth.

"Mommy! Wake up!" Kaleigha squirmed, but I pinned her against me, turning out of my own mother's grip.

"Daddy! Help, Mommy!" Kaleigha pleaded. The tension in my throat made breathing impossible, much less speaking.

When we left the worship center, I heard a man's sobs, like something you'd hear in a sad movie—Charlie. Donna's sobs came next. Keeping my gaze on the concrete floor of the atrium, I put Kaleigha down. "Go with Grandma." I pointed to Mom, not even glancing at Dad.

Bella reached for me from Kelly's arms. "Mama," she garbled.

I took her into my arms.

"You okay?" Kelly put a hand on my shoulder, her voice hoarse.

I felt Bella curl into my shoulder, holding her only with one arm as I covered my face with my other hand, shaking my head.

"Breathe," Kelly said to me. "Austin, take in a deep breath." She did this with me, her chest rising and lowering slowly. We breathed again in sync a few more times.

Chris and Megan walked through the doors; his arm was wrapped around her shoulders.

"Hey," Chris said.

"Hey." I cleared my throat, pinching my nose, smiling at them through my watery eyes.

They both came over to Kelly and me.

"How are you doing?" Chris whispered.

Shifting Bella so she could see Chris, I considered how to respond as he gave my arm a nudge with his knuckles. "Eh." I just traced my smooth jawline.

Megan and Kelly wept in their embrace. Their small, quiet sobs threatened me to do the same. I put a light hand on Megan's cardigan, acknowledging her, and that was when she invited Chris and me to join them. Unwilling to drown in a flood of tears, I pulled away, sighing. Chris's face faded into a pigment of bright pink.

It didn't take long for others to start showing up. In a twisted way, it felt like a meet and greet. While people would cry at meet and greets, it was never about things that affected me personally. Usually, when people cried, it would be like, "This song got me through a really tough time." That would definitely hit, but the occasional "This song saved my life" would hit even harder, because it would remind us why we spent time away from our wives and kids.

But this wasn't a meet and greet. This wasn't a wedding. This wasn't a reunion. This was a visitation for a wife, mother, daughter, sister, friend, missionary, and role model. This was a visitation for a twenty-six-year-old who wouldn't even get to see her babies go to school.

This was devastating. I knew it, but I intentionally tried not to process it or think too hard about it, because I just needed to get through the funeral, which led to me to ask people about what was going on in their lives instead.

Keaton, our former keys player, walked in. Naturally blond and tall, his confident demeanor was its own introduction. He wore a navy button-down shirt and khaki jeans.

"Hey," he interrupted a surface-level conversation I was having with a guy, Dillon, from the label.

"Keaton!" I said, genuinely excited to see him. Even with Bella in my arms, he went in for a full embrace.

When I pulled away, he whispered, "I'm so sorry." I'd never seen him this emotional before.

"Thank you, Keaton."

"She's the second one?" He put a light hand on Bella's back, who buried her face in my chest.

"She is."

He cleared his throat. "How are the girls doing?"

"They . . . they're okay. How's seminary?" I asked him.

"It's good. Time consuming though."

"Did you fly in today?"

"Yeah, I literally just came from the airport."

"Thank you so much for flying out here."

"Yeah, of course. I knew her very well."

"I know." I wanted to change the subject. "You're staying with Tennyson and Elena?"

"Yeah." I couldn't ask him about his fiancée because they'd broken up. Tennyson would've been his best man, so Keaton had called him to let us know. Riley, Chris, and I were also going to be in the wedding. Tennyson hadn't really known what had happened.

"You think you're gonna go back on tour?" he asked me.

"We don't know yet," I said quietly, knowing people in our circle, especially from the label, stood within eavesdropping distance.

"What do you think you're gonna do?"

"Hopefully, go back on the road, but logistically, I don't know."

Throughout the evening, I held Bella close, held back a lot of tears, said thank you, gave sad smiles, and hugged more people than I could count, overwhelmed by the support for our family. A lot of Christian music people, big and small names alike, came to support both Kelly and me.

Toward the end of the night, the lead singer from Cara's favorite band approached us. GreenButton was her second favorite band. If she could've known he would come to her visitation, she would've figured out a way to rise from the dead.

"Oh, hey," I said to him with forced enthusiasm, my voice dry from talking an extensive amount that evening.

"Hey, I'm so sorry for your loss, man," he told me, clasping my hand and then patting my back.

"Thank you," I told him. "You guys are—you guys were her favorite band. This would mean everything to her."

Giving me a sad smile, he sighed. "Well, on the other side, we'll let her know I was here, deal?" He was serious.

Nodding, I grappled with the tension of wanting to be with Jesus and bringing Heaven here. Jesus did not come to Earth to make us want to leave Earth. He came to bring Heaven to Earth, and He showed us how to also bring Heaven here by loving people and loving God. Where was Cara? I didn't know—sure, wherever

Heaven was, but I had no idea *what* Heaven was. Could I dare to ask the question: was Heaven simply dying? Was there really an afterlife? I pushed these questions away, as they provided no comfort. In fact, such questions put my already jeopardized career in even more jeopardy, even with the GoFundMe abundantly funded.

That night, after I put the girls down with Mom's help, I decided to hide out in the studio where I had blown up an air mattress. My parents stayed in the guest bedroom. I thought about trying to write, but I didn't want to cry.

* * *

Shutting the casket wasn't something I had been prepared for. I'd never see her again. On that Wednesday night, when we had left Nashville, I could never have dreamt that would be the last time I'd look into her aquamarine eyes.

Chris walked up onto the stage with a Bible in his hands. He set it on the podium and took in a deep breath, staring down at the holy book. "If someone told me a week ago I'd be giving a eulogy for Cara, I would not have believed them, and I know I'm not the only one who's still in shock. But I'm also . . . devastated. I'm saddened by the fact that someone as sweet, kind, and loving as Cara no longer gets to light up dark moments directly. I'm saddened that she won't get to watch her kids grow up. Or meet her grandkids. I feel for her parents, Donna and Charlie. I feel for her sister, Kelly. I feel for her husband, Austin. I feel for my wife, Megan, one of her best friends. I feel for all her friends. I feel for the people who look up to her. I feel it myself because I feel like I lost a sister, so getting through this eulogy is going to be tough. Getting through the next season is going to be tough, too." His voice was already gone. I knew he was going to cry. I toyed with my wedding ring.

"I first met Cara in 2008 when we were playing a music festival in Michigan. GreenButton, the band I'm a part of, had just signed a record deal, and we were beginning to travel the country. Cara was Kelly Minty's sister, there to help her big sister out by selling merchandise. I noticed right away she was unashamedly herself in her own way: soft-spoken but bold. She was an ambitious college student, majoring in accounting, yet wanting to eventually be a missionary." He took in a deep breath, struggling with words all of a sudden. "And she followed that dream." His voice broke during that sentence. Sitting between both Donna and Kelly, I saw them wipe their tears with tissues in my peripheral vision as I stared down at my knees.

Continuing, Chris's voice evened out. "Cara was the kind of person who lived out grace. She knew who her hope was in. She knew she was loved by God; therefore, she wanted every single person she interacted with to know they were loved by God, too. It came out in the way she treated people on a daily basis. She loved her kids. She loved Austin. She loved her friends and family well, always putting them first. She even loved strangers well. Loving well also means showing grace. When she would discipline Kaleigha or Bella, she would never scold. Stern, sure, but kind and empathetic.

"When I was only dating my wife, Megan, we found out we were pregnant with twins. I had to tell Austin, and I was worried our music would be dropped from the radio, that we'd get kicked off tour, and it would be my fault for getting a girl pregnant out of wedlock. In my mind, I thought I'd need to quit and figure out another job, because I would have to support Megan and not one, but two kids. As I was telling Austin everything, I started crying, because I was scared. Then Cara walked out, saw me, and asked if I needed a hug before even asking me what was wrong. When I told her I had gotten Megan pregnant, she asked, 'Are those happy tears?' I told her, 'No. I'm going to get the band kicked off Christian radio. I might have to quit.' She looked at me, and said, 'The only reason you'd get kicked off Christian radio would be because you forgot that God's grace is bigger than anything.'" He paused to swallow. "'And you're going to be a great father.'"

Chris rarely talked about getting Megan pregnant, especially not in front of anyone from the label.

My mind wandered to the label. Would they take our record deal away?—because I wouldn't be touring at least for a while. Probably. My mind spiraled with questions about the future. Would I ever get to tour again? How would I do it without Cara? I was the only living parent to my kids.

The next thing I knew, we were lowering my wife into the ground. Her body was dead. The Cara I knew was dead. My dad had driven Mom and me to the cemetery. I had been quiet on the way to the funeral that morning and on the way to the burial, but I had absolutely no words on the way to the church for the luncheon. It was a silence I had never experienced before.

When we got there, my throat wouldn't accept food. I almost threw up when I took a bite of my egg salad sandwich.

"You're not eating much," Mom noticed, catching me in the act as I sat back down.

"Yeah, I'm not hungry," I lied. Over the last few days, I hadn't eaten much, but I physically could not that afternoon.

We had to stay around and thank people for coming, even though I wanted to hide.

When we finally got back to the house, the babysitter left, and I changed out of the suit and tie I'd been suffocating in. That meant going into our bedroom, through the bathroom, in order to get to the closet. Walking in quickly, I shut the door between me and the bedroom, heading to the closet to change into a faded kelly green crew neck sweatshirt that Cara had bought me. Most of my clothes were bought by Cara, my mom, or other women in my family. It was strange being in my house on a Thursday, changing in the middle of the day.

When I walked back into the bathroom, I caught sight of myself in the mirror. There were bags underneath my eyes. I'd aged at least five years.

Staring at my silver wedding ring, I questioned if I should take it off. Letting my eyes well up, telling myself I didn't have to fight it, I debated whether I was ready to let go, remembering my parents were downstairs and Kaleigha was always scampering around nearby. The chances of one of them barging in were pretty high, so I continued to hold back tears as I played with the ring, keeping it below my knuckle. It was a symbol of our marriage. Even if I wanted to run from the vibrant memories of the last six years of knowing her, I couldn't.

And I didn't really see how this would ever get better. Everything I had worked for—suddenly shattered. We couldn't get back on the road very easily. I didn't have a college degree. I had no idea what I was going to do. Although an undeserved

GoFundMe account would provide us flexibility for a little while, I didn't want to mope around being unproductive because I didn't want to dwell in the ringing silence of not having her around.

The one thing I loved to do seemed out of reach with her gone. What was I going to write? Praise songs? The idea of writing songs about the questions burning inside of me just seemed . . . draining. I didn't want music to be the thing that would break me; it was the only thing that had ever kept me together. And Cara. I blinked the tears back into my eyes. Crying seemed like a lot of work.

Walking out of the bathroom, I sat on the tile of the fireplace. Cara loved the fireplace of our master bedroom, even though I had never gotten around to setting it up to work; I never would now. I stared at the bed, ashamed of the disappointment that came with being suddenly and involuntarily celibate. Leaning against the fireplace, I asked God, *Why?* and told Him, *You could've stopped this*. His immediate response of, *"I love You and I will never forsake You"* pissed me off.

When a knock came to my door, I found my voice: "Come in."

Dad looked around, probably expecting to find me in the bed or chair.

"Hey," he said.

"Hi." The one-syllable word took every ounce of my being to utter.

He came over and sat next to me. Even with the fireplace empty, the pores in my face prickled. "You okay?"

Taking in a deep breath, I stared at the bland carpet and shook my head, holding back my tears again, pinching my chin as it threatened to reveal a mind of its own.

"What can I do?"

He wasn't oblivious to how torn up I felt, and we sat for a moment because I didn't trust my voice.

Eventually, I managed, "I mean, you can help me move."

"Deal." He gave me a hand to shake. I shook it.

"Where's Daddy?" I heard Kaleigha ask Mom.

"I don't know," Mom answered.

"I'm gonna find him."

I rubbed my nose. "I'm on duty," I mumbled to him.

"You don't have to be."

Her little feet scampered up the stairs.

"No, it's fine. She's a good distraction," I admitted, sniffing.

He squeezed my knee. "Okay."

When Kaleigha ran into my room, I opened my arms, not in the mood to talk but to hold her.

"Daddy! Park!"

It was a gloomy day, more suited for a funeral than a playground. "How are you going to get there?" I teased, almost too relaxed.

"I drive!" she informed me.

The thought of Kaleigha driving? *Oh, Lord, help us.* "Oh, okay. Well, if you can pick me up, we can go to the park."

Of course, she tried, by putting her hands up my armpits. "Wet."

I giggled, either because of her little hands tickling me or her innocent bluntness. I ran a hand through my hair to get it out of my face.

"You look funny," she told me, maybe due to my red face.

"Why?" I asked her. "Because I do this?" I made the goofiest face I could and messed up my hair until it stuck out in every direction.

That made her giggle, too, as I sniffed, pinching my nose, smirking at her. Picking her up as I stood, she leaned against my chest. "Let's look outside, okay?"

I pulled the window coverings up, revealing the fluffy gray clouds. We looked down at our deck.

"Rain," she groaned.

"Yeah," I told her sadly, but content with the idea of staying in. I was exhausted. I wasn't worried about today as much but in general. How was I supposed to keep this kid entertained for the next decade? I wanted to ask her what she wanted to do, but I didn't want to have to tell her no.

Dad stood up, too, folding his arms.

"No rain!" She pleaded with the window, her chin trembling as I set her down on the bed, sitting next to her, turning to face her.

"What did you want to do at the park?" *Let's get creative.*

"Slide." She scowled, folding her arms.

We had stairs—although my parents would likely report me to Children's Services if I used the stairs as a slide. But if I held her on the way down, I would take the hit instead of her if things were to go south. She'd love it. My mom and dad would think I had lost it, but oh well.

I picked her up and said, "I have a plan." I walked her out of my bedroom, itching my eyes. My whole body felt overheated, but I powered through. When we got to the top of the stairs, I sat down, shifting her to a sitting position on my lap as I wrapped my arms around her stomach. "Okay, hang on tight." I glanced at Dad who had followed us out. Just going for it, I let my legs go and used my hand to push myself. Kaleigha giggled all the way down the stairs.

Mom jumped to her feet immediately, greeting us at the bottom with Bella in her arms. Her eyes widened through her glasses, perhaps convinced I had fully gone insane.

Dad announced, "I want a turn!"

"You wanna sit on my lap?" I asked Dad.

"I think I'm good, Austin." His tone was assertive.

Kaleigha ran back up the stairs, beaming as if plopping down fifteen steps was the best thing she had ever done.

The better sight was Dad sliding down the stairs, still in his dress pants, his royal blue tie flying to keep up with him. For nearly an hour, we experienced the newly discovered playground of the home Cara and I had created a family in. Bella loved it even more than Kaleigha. Even Mom, the engineering professor, changed into more comfortable clothes to join in. Now that was a sight.

6

SAM

"So, do you think we'll ever tour again?" I asked Chris as he leaned against the closed door of my condo.

"I'm not sure," Chris said.

"But what do you think is gonna happen?"

"I think . . ." The scruff on his face scratched his hand. "I think it's . . . up in the air. I don't know. Austin's a single parent now, and being a single parent and being on tour doesn't exactly add up." He sighed. "But we'll know more after the meeting next week."

"You don't think we'll go back on tour," I mumbled, unable to mask the disappointment in my voice.

Twisting his golden ring around his finger, he glanced down at me. "I don't know, Sam."

"Like, what do you actually think?" I pleaded, folding my arms against my ribs.

Placing a hand on the doorknob, he put his other hand in his pocket. "I mean, I . . . I think it all depends on what Austin wants to do." Then he said under his breath, "And the label."

"I just—I guess I want to know if I need to start applying to jobs or colleges or what." I put my hands up.

"Well," he said, "slow down." He put both of his hands up. "The GoFundMe thing was funded for us to take time off, so you don't need to know right away."

"I know, but if we're going to break up, I need to start figuring things out."

"But why?" He sounded curious, not accusatory.

"Because—I don't—I'm already—I should be a junior in college right now, and . . . I'm already behind."

"Since when did you wanna go to college?" he asked.

"Since the band decided it might fall apart."

"Nothing's been decided, man." Chris paused. "But what would you study?"

"I honestly don't even know."

"So, why would you go to college if you don't know what you'd want to study in the first place?"

Stuffing my hands into the pockets of my shorts, I admitted, "Because my parents' will was set up so that I can't access the money until I'm twenty-six or graduated from college."

Chris inhaled what I'd said. "So, you're not sure what you're going to do once the GoFundMe money runs out?"

Nodding, I stared over at the blurred TV, now paused on the Netflix show I'd been watching until Chris came to drop off a CD. As my bottom lip started to tremble, I bit my cracked lip, tearing the peeling skin with my teeth.

"It makes sense why you're so anxious," he said. "And I get that there's a lot of uncertainty right now, and I can only imagine what it's like to not have your parents, but it's going to be okay. I can promise you Megan and I won't let you starve, okay?"

"Thanks." My voice sounded off. I asked him one more time, "But really, do you think we're not going back on tour?"

"Sam, I love you, but I don't know. I want to know, too, but I don't." He used the same tone he probably would use with his kids. I let my eyes flutter back tears, still not filtering out the frustration, unable to meet his eyes. "Hey," he whispered. "I know it's tough, but it's going to be okay."

Swallowing back tears, tasting the mucus in my throat, I nodded. It would be fine.

"You good?" he asked.

I sighed. I hated that he asked me that because he knew the answer, and I didn't know how to respond. I couldn't be emotional in front of him. It had become an unspoken rule that I wouldn't talk about my parents around people and they wouldn't bring it up.

"Whatcha thinking about?" he asked.

"Honestly, I thought the band was my redemption story, and now Cara is dead; it's going to impact everything." My voice rose until it cracked as I pushed back tears by staring at the ceiling, slapping my thigh.

"I know," he said quietly, putting his hands on his hips.

I focused on slow, deep breaths; I wanted him to leave.

"I'm sorry," I said, deepening my voice. "That was a lot."

"No, *you're* fine." His voice sounded confident, albeit uneven. "I'm just sorry you have to deal with everything at twenty years old."

"It's not your fault." I tasted blood from my lips. "I really don't know what to do."

"Yeah, I guess we don't get to know right now, and yet all you can do is trust that God is bigger than the uncertainty and the pain."

"That's easier said than done."

"Yeah, and God is bigger than your inability to feel like He's bigger." He wrapped an arm around me as I wiped my nose with the back of my hand.

When he left, I went to my room and cried.

7

CHRIS

"How are you holding up?" I asked Austin as I sat at his kitchen island. His kids were asleep upstairs, and it was chillingly quiet in the house.

"I'm holding up," he told me. "You want a Mountain Dew?" Cara had always kept them on hand just for me.

"Um, yeah." I smiled at him.

"How does caffeine not affect us?" Austin asked.

"It's not like I can fall asleep until midnight anyway." I chuckled.

"I feel that." He took a Mountain Dew out of his fridge, tossing it to me.

"Whoa!" I barely caught it. "You're really trusting." I stared at him, my eyes as wide as my circular glasses.

"Is it bad that part of me wanted to see it explode?" he asked me.

"Um." I looked at him, sliding my glasses back up the bridge of my nose. "To be honest, there was a tiny part of me that wanted to see that, too."

"It would've probably woken up the girls," he told me.

"Yeah, we wouldn't have wanted that."

"You would've been the one to calm them down to make up for your butterfingers."

Raising my eyebrows, I accused, "Oh, so it would've been my fault?"

"Yup." Genuine amusement filled his eyes—a refreshing sight. "All your fault." He gave me a smile.

"I'm gonna wait to open this now." I set it on the counter.

He nodded. "That's probably wise."

"So, how are things?"

"Okay." His eyes were blue marbles staring at the double doors that led to the sunroom.

"What does 'okay' mean?"

Popping open his Dr. Pepper, he admitted, "I'm kinda stressed at the moment."

"You wanna elaborate?"

"So, basically, Nate talked to the label, and Dillon basically said if we're not back on the road by Labor Day, they're gonna revoke our contract."

Glaring at the Mountain Dew can, I folded my arms. "Okay, that pisses me off. Your wife just died, and the label knows that most of the GoFundMe money is going to them to pay for time lost."

"Yeah, I know, and it's not like we had a huge life insurance policy for a twenty-six-year-old."

I scanned the kitchen, noting the sparkly black table and dark woodwork of Austin and Cara's home, trying to take in the memories we had made here, aware that Austin would be moving soon. Across from me, Austin still wore his silver wedding band. "So, what are you wanting to do?"

"I don't even know," he grumbled. "I guess we get back on the road as soon as we can."

"How soon is soon?"

"I mean, technically we could finish the tour out with Resin Ring." Austin twisted his square green earring.

"What about your kids?"

"Donna and Charlie could watch them."

"For how long?"

"Whenever we're on the road."

"You're for sure wanting to go back on the road?"

"Yeah, for now." He twisted his ring on his finger, taking a sip of his Dr. Pepper. "Do you think that's bad?"

"Why would it be bad?"

"Because I have kids at home, and I—I'm their only parent, and if I'm not there . . ." Running out of breath, he took another sip of his Dr. Pepper.

I clasped his forearm for a moment. "I can't tell you what's best for your family."

"I know." He walked away from the counter, over to the sunroom, flipping on a light. "But what would you do, Chris?"

"Honestly, man, I would pray about it." I followed him into the sunroom, grabbing my unopened pop.

"I have."

"And?"

He looked down. "I can't tell. I go back and forth on what I think He's saying."

"What do you mean?" In the glass we faced, our reflections stared back at us.

"I don't even know," he told me, sitting down on one of the couches. "Like, I want to go back on tour, but I don't—I don't know if it's the right thing to do. But I don't know what else I would do." He cleared his throat. "We can't afford to take time off, especially if I wanna move."

"Don't you need to take time off if you wanna move?" I challenged, sitting in the chair closest to him.

Granting me a smile, he said, "I mean, yes, but financially, we need to be on the road."

"That's fair. Are you serious about this?"

Austin placed the Dr. Pepper on the clear glass table. "I don't know." He stared at his reflection. "I literally don't know what to do, Chris. I've thought about moving back to Iowa and working for my dad at the insurance company, but if I did that, I would be committing to giving up music."

I had no idea what to tell him, so I asked, "What would Cara encourage you to do?"

Leaning back on the couch, stretching his legs out, he took a sip of his pop, and when he didn't talk, I noticed his eyes were watering. I waited. He wore his red Iowa State jacket; the green earring clashed with the red. Then he stuffed his hands into his pockets as he leaned back again. "I think she'd probably encourage me to go back on tour."

"You think she would?"

"Yeah, she understood . . ." His voice started to bend as he shook his head, staring straight ahead, blinking back tears, so I studied the can of Mountain Dew.

I debated whether I should crack open the can. It'd probably be fine. There was no rug on the tile, but as much as I wanted to see him laugh, I owed it to him to sit in this pain.

Austin continued, "I just—I don't know if it's fair to Kaleigha and Bella to be raised by their grandparents."

It wasn't fair they didn't have a mom either.

"What's best for your kids?" I asked.

"Cara," he mumbled.

"You and Cara were rock stars together."

Wincing, he clenched his jaw. His index finger moved from his upper to lower lip as if to remove tension knots from his lips.

I waited for him to say something.

"I don't want my kids to think I don't want to be around them, especially now, but I also don't want to be a quitter." He swallowed. "I'm still wearing this earring, so maybe that's a sign."

"If the earring had fallen out a year ago, would you have quit the band?"

He smiled. "I'd pray about it and assess the situation." He looked at me. "I'm not set on touring forever, but I would love to do it as long as we can do it well."

"Do you think the earring is a distraction, or a symbol from the Holy Spirit?"

"I mean, what path allows me to love better?"

"You tell me."

"Does being gone, given the circumstances, equate to me not loving them well?"

"No, Austin. Not even close. You not loving them well would be you not taking care of yourself."

"I'm trying," he told me.

"You're doing a pretty good job."

"I don't know about that," he said under his breath.

A hollowness shot through my stomach, imbedding a golf ball in my throat. "Why do you say that?"

"Kaleigha and Bella want their mama, and I don't know how to help them, because they want her."

"How often does that happen?"

"Every day." He cleared his throat, twisting the ring on his finger again; I wondered if he even realized he was doing it. "And Bella's obviously too young to understand Cara is not coming back. Kaleigha sort of gets it, but not exactly why—not that I do either." He shook his head. "Anyway, what were we talking about? Tour?"

I put a hand up. "Hold on, how are you handling taking care of the girls on your own?"

"Um, I mean, it's confusing for them, because she was away on the mission trip, and then she came back, so Kaleigha will randomly talk about how Mommy is going to come back and play house, and I'm like . . ."

When he swallowed his words, I found my eyes welling up, too. It sunk in. Cara wasn't coming back. Austin and his family knew it. Megan knew it. I knew it.

With his elbow on the armrest, he rested his cheek on his fist, looking at the tan paint of the wall. "I hate having to tell Kaleigha over and over again that Cara's not coming back. Trying to explain that is impossible."

"How do you?"

"You try to explain God. Heaven. Basically, I remind her that God is holding the earth and all the people in it, and He made the stars and the moon and the sun. I tell her that He loves and cares about everyone, but our bodies will all stop working at some point, which means we can't stay on Earth. And I tell her that because God wants us to live forever, because He wants to be with us, we get new bodies in Heaven—where Mommy's at."

"That's a beautiful picture of the gospel."

Austin swallowed. "I try."

Nonchalantly, I pinched my eyes underneath my glasses.

"You good?" he asked.

"No," I told him. "I cannot even imagine having to tell Catherine and Candy that if Megan died, but your faith is inspiring, Austin." My broken voice reminded me how much her loss was affecting me, too, as I wiped my eyes again.

"It is what it is." His voice was strained.

Picking up the Mountain Dew, I sniffled. "Do you think it will explode?"

"Only one way to find out."

Opening it, slowly and carefully, I heard it fizz, feeling the tension of the metal. I cracked the metal and flinched. Nothing happened. Cautiously, I lifted it to take a sip of the fizzy drink.

"Good job. So graceful."

"Thank you. Thank you."

"We need to go back on tour," he told me.

"Okay." I held my breath. "You think you can get through a set?"

"I think so. I guess we'll find out."

"Can you sing if you're emotional?" I leaned in, anticipating his answer.

"I . . ." He looked at me. "Yes?" He gave me a smile. "But I'll try to avoid getting emotional."

"Would you talk about Cara during a set?"

"I don't know. Probably not. What would I say? 'By the way, my wife died.'"

"I mean, you could talk about how the promise of the cross keeps you going through this, but you don't have to."

"I could, but then I *might* cry on stage, so how about not?"

"Fair enough."

8

TENNYSON

"What did you find out from the meeting?" Elena asked me, cutting carrots in the kitchen as Joshua, our kid, stood right next to her.

"Hey, buddy." I ruffled his light blond hair. "We're going to do a few shows this summer, and then we're going back on tour in the fall." I slid off my shoes, walking over to wrap my arms around my wife's chest, kissing her blonde hair.

"Full time?" she asked.

"Yeah."

She continued chopping carrots as I loosened my grip. "How can Austin go back on tour?"

"Cara's parents are going to watch the kids." She didn't say anything as I grabbed a cup from the cupboard. "What?" I asked her as I filled the cup in the sink; we hadn't invested in a fridge with a water dispenser.

"I never imagined y'all would go back on the road right away."

"What do you mean?"

Joshua followed me.

"Austin shouldn't be away from his kids." Elena paused. "How is Austin, anyway?"

"I don't know." Taking a sip of water, I added, "It's hard to tell, to be honest. He wanted to finish the tour with Resin Ring, but they'd already pulled the shows."

"He tried to go back on tour with Resin Ring? Like, this spring?" Her eyes widened.

"Yeah."

"Are you serious?"

"Yup."

"He thought that was an option?"

"I guess. Nate was like, 'Bro, use the funding.'"

"Sounds like he's in denial."

"Probably."

"How do you *think* Austin's doing?" she asked quietly.

Putting the cup on the counter, I looked at her apprehensive expression. "I don't know. Do you want me to call him up and ask him?" I said sarcastically.

"I mean, yeah, maybe, if you don't know. He is one of your best friends."

"I'm not gonna do that. He's okay."

Joshua lifted up his arms, so I picked him up.

"His wife just died, Tennyson. He's probably not okay."

Putting a hand up, I said, "Okay, then he's not okay." Why was she asking then?

"You know it wouldn't hurt to ask the people around you how they are every once in a while," she mumbled.

I understood what she was getting at. "How are you, Elena?" I tried to not make that question sound like a chore.

"My good friend died, and my husband is going back on tour, and he didn't even ask me." She stopped cutting the carrots, setting down the knife before turning toward me.

"I didn't know that we were on different pages with that. I'm sorry."

"Shouldn't this be a wake-up call to be around the people you love?"

Joshua gazed at Elena, taking in the moment. "Believe me, it is, but the main reason we're going back is to avoid being indebted to the label. To keep our record deal. It's stupid—I know."

"You know they can find another drummer to tour with." She moved on to cutting up tomatoes.

"Elena," I exclaimed. "Come on, this is my job."

"Yeah, but no one is making you tour!" I hadn't realized I'd raised my voice until she mirrored mine. "There are other jobs, Tennyson."

"There are, but this is what I do. I mean, things are already stressful enough. Me quitting right now would only make it worse."

"Okay, but if you're not going back on the road until summer, then they have time to figure something else out."

"Elena," I said quietly, remembering Joshua was in my arms as he played with my sweatshirt strings, whimpering slightly. "It's okay, buddy," I whispered to him.

"I want you home." Warmth flooded her words, her eyes welling up.

Maybe I didn't know how Austin was doing. If it had been Elena?—man, I didn't even want to go there. Suddenly, I found my arm around her, pulling her into me. "I'm not super fired up about leaving you guys, and I . . ." My chest tightened as she put the knife down to hug me. Her baggy gray sweatshirt and square black glasses made her even cuter. I kissed her silky blonde hair.

"You don't have to go."

"It's the right thing to do."

She pulled away to meet my eyes. "Is it?" Tears fell out behind her glasses, and she put her hand over her face under her glasses to wipe them quickly.

I swallowed. "I'm gonna be honest."

"Okay . . ." She raised her blonde eyebrows.

"I don't want the last memory of tour to be finding out Cara died."

We didn't say anything for a moment.

"That's valid." She pulled Joshua and me into another embrace, and I pulled away when my face grew warm. She put a hand on my chest.

"I just—I don't want you to think I don't care," I said. "Or that I'm not considering what you're going through. I know this is even harder on you."

"I don't think that. And I know this isn't easy for you either. You toured with her for a year and a half." Her voice quivered with every word.

Putting Joshua down because he was starting to squirm, I took another sip of the water. "I literally hate everything about this," I told her, not expecting the anger in my voice.

"I know." She calmed her voice.

"I just . . ." I didn't even know how to answer that, so I pressed my lips together. My chest rose unevenly as I attempted a smile. I whispered to her, groaning, "It's not fair to anyone. Literally, the label doesn't care about us. Or Austin. If he could be home with his kids, I bet he would, but we're pretty locked in right now. At least he is."

She kissed my cheek, wrapping an arm around my back. "What about you? Can you quit?"

"Not right now. I wouldn't feel right about quitting right now."

"But eventually?"

"Yes," I promised.

9

AUSTIN

Kelly took my headphones off as I sat down on the stool next to her, still not used to the setup of the studio in my new house. Kelly's unnaturally wavy black hair was tied with a thin, clear band into a ponytail, resting against her oversized golden crop top, her lower back revealed.

Watching her eyes outlined by thick black eyeliner, I noticed the light layer of foundation sparkle over her face, almost like tiny crystals ingrained in a fresh blanket of snow. Her dark green eyes grew glossy.

"Well, what did you think?" I folded my arms.

"I'm loving what you did with the bridge. The clarity of your voice makes it shine." Then she grabbed my forearm, her hands cold. "But that was the most surface level song you've ever written."

"It is not," I said confidently.

"I feel like you're just . . ." She sighed, pressing her thick pink lips together. "I feel like this is like when someone asks you how you are and you say, 'I'm okay,' but you don't really mean it. It's rehearsed. Uninspired."

"Okay, Kelly." I glared at her, hearing the amused defense in my tone. "What do you want me to write about?"

"Something that's not so jaded."

"What do you mean, 'jaded'?"

"I want you to stop pretending like everything's fine."

"I'm not, Kelly." My voice cracked, annoyed she would accuse me of being inauthentic.

"Yeah, but how often do you talk about it, Austin?"

"Talk about what, Kelly?"

"You know what," she snapped. "Cara."

"What do you want me to say about her?"

"I want you to keep her memory alive."

"I try, Kelly." I sighed, folding my arms. "I try to live as she did by loving people well and showing grace to others." A burning sensation of yearning inflamed my chest. Kelly squeezed my shoulder, and I offered a smile. "I'm not perfect at it though." Just today, I'd snapped at Kaleigha when she hadn't wanted me to brush her hair. Cara had been so much better at parenting.

"She wasn't perfect either, and she really leaned into Jesus in those moments."

"I know." I took in a few deep breaths, pinching my nose.

"What are you thinking about?"

"It's been a rough day."

"Why?"

"I yelled at Kaleigha after bath time when she didn't want me to brush her hair, and she cried, and I hope I don't hurt her when

I comb her hair." I swallowed, resisting the urge to cry as I rubbed my chin with my thumb.

"You don't. Little girls don't always like getting their hair combed."

I stared down at my dark blue jeans, and then she wrapped an arm around me, likely unsure of how to respond.

"What are you thinking about?" Kelly asked again.

I shrugged. "I also set the spaghetti on fire tonight."

"Legitimately?"

"Yeah."

"That's why it smells in here."

"Can you actually smell it?"

"Yeah, I didn't know if it was just your new house or what."

Groaning, I mumbled, "Nope."

"How do you even catch spaghetti on fire?" She raised her eyebrows, containing her laughter.

"I forgot to put the water in."

"Austin!" She started laughing out loud.

"It's not funny." But I was laughing. "I almost burned the house down, Kelly!"

"Okay, but you didn't."

"Can you imagine that news story?" I asked her. "Singer of GreenButton burns house down because he doesn't know how to cook." I deepened my voice, in a lame attempt to sound like a news anchor.

She lost it by squealing into a high, extensive howl. "I'm sorry. I shouldn't laugh," she somehow managed to say. Then she hiccupped.

I clutched my stomach that began to cramp from laughing so hard, pretending to glare at her. The image of spaghetti catching on fire was burned into my mind. Everything was fine now, but in the moment? It had been terrifying. Kelly's snorts and hiccups made me laugh so hard to the point where my eyes were watering about something unrelated to Cara.

When we stopped laughing, her eyes caught mine. "Other than almost burning down your new house, how are things?"

Nodding, I shrugged, "They're . . ." I didn't know how to dance around the question. "There's a lot going on, but nothing at all, all at once."

"Like, taking care of two kids and trying to get back on tour?"

"I need to get back on tour."

Kelly nodded. "I know you want to." She looked at me. "But in order to do that, you need to do more writing—writing that's real." She softened her voice. "Maybe you should write about being overwhelmed."

"I'm sorry." I squeezed my quivering lips with my index finger and thumb.

"You know it's okay to cry?"

"I know, I know."

"Do you though?"

"I don't know." I twisted my ring, hating how I always fidgeted with it. "I wasn't much of a crier. Cara never saw me cry."

"Never?" Her neck jolted in my direction.

"Never."

"Oh, wow." She wrapped a hand around my wrist. "Not even tear up?"

"Um, maybe. That didn't even happen very often."

"What was the most upset she ever saw you?" Her voice grew higher as if she were talking to Kaleigha.

I thought about it. When she was in my life, things were going well—not that everything was perfect. We weren't perfect. Our relationship wasn't perfect. But we chose each other. Maybe she'd chosen me more than I'd chosen her, which I hated myself for. "There were some really hard nights to hit the road, like when the girls had the stomach flu, and I still had to leave. And when my grandma passed away."

"Were you close with your grandma?"

Shrugging, I bit the inside of my lip. "When I lived in Iowa, we were close. She died pretty suddenly, so it was hard." I shifted my position, uncrossing my legs, resting my bare feet on the ragged carpet, the only downside of the new house. If Cara had lived here, she probably would've demanded we get new carpet because of the random stains. Instead, I had the carpet shampooed. It was very soft, almost too soft—grimy even. It was clean, at least?

"What do you think Cara would say to you now if she was still here?"

I hated that question. I got it a lot.

I didn't know the answer, but I felt her presence at that moment. I felt her love, despite the fact she wasn't with me. Knowing what it felt like to be loved and supported by someone as genuine as Cara reminded me to show that love to others.

"She'd probably tell me it's going to be okay and point me back to the promise and hope of the cross."

Kelly nodded, pressing her lips together. Her dark green eyes held tears. Taking in her beauty, I wondered what would happen if we were to date. And then I felt like a horrible person, especially because she was with Riley. And because she was Cara's sister.

"She would point you back to Jesus."

"I should write a tribute song for her that explains the gospel and how it sets us free."

"You totally should. I'll help if you want."

We wrote the song in twenty minutes. That wasn't planned, but our inspiration made it easy. We were proud of what we'd written. Our voices blended together in perfect harmony.

I still see her face in everything
But life goes on at a rapid pace
A sharp blade of reality
Makes me wonder if I took her all in vain,
Bleeding in the pain
Not strong enough to try
Too ashamed to cry
And all I can do is mope
Can barely speak
Cuts so deep
But I don't wanna weep
Sleep my only refuge
Unless I'm dreaming about her
Bittersweet dreams
Playin' tricks on my mind
Trust issues, hope found, hope lost
In the moments I can't see
Your grace still remains bigger
Than the wars inside my mind
You are still good

You are still kind
I will live with the hope of the cross
As I begin to cope
But if You could do anything, God
I don't understand why
You would let her go so soon?
I know this pain is temporary
And maybe she's just asleep
In the mourning, You will weep with me
Until the morning light
This is the good fight
That I don't have to fight alone
Because You are bigger than
My questions and my doubts
About You being big enough
You are bigger than my lack of trust
You are bigger than my inability
To comprehend Your grace and love

We recorded the demo. As we listened to it, I grew misty. Kelly shed a few tears. It was the first time since Cara passed away that I felt excited and proud of something I'd written.

"I want this to be a single," Kelly told me.

"Me too." I rubbed my nose.

"I'm gonna send it to Grayson Clay." Grayson was a producer, songwriter, and mutual friend.

"You totally should."

"I will tomorrow, after I dye my hair," she said.

"Oh, yeah?" I raised my eyebrows. "What color?"

"I'm gonna do maroon and blue highlights with the hope they fade into pink and teal."

"I'm actually gonna dye my hair blond." I smirked, not meaning it.

"You mean, bleach it?" she corrected.

"Um, sure?"

"When you lighten your hair, you're bleaching and toning it."

"Toning it? What does that mean?"

"When people bleach their hair from a dark color, it usually comes out as a brassy or yellow-blond, so people will tone it to cool it down."

That kind of went over my head. "Cara was a real blonde, right?" I thought out loud.

"No, she bleached it."

"She did not."

"She totally did," she countered. "It was her little secret."

"Shut up," I told her, chuckling uncomfortably. Kelly was making me question how well I'd known my wife. She was messing with me, *right?*

"She was really lucky to have natural light blonde hair."

"What's your real color?"

"Like a very, very dirty blonde, or light brown. It's honestly a really ugly color."

"Now, I doubt that." I rolled my eyes.

"No, really, it looks so bad with my pale skin."

"So, what made you choose black?"

"I like the contrast."

"You like looking emo." I smirked, glancing at her golden top.

"Oh, yeah, *so* emo." She batted her eyes—dark green eyes. Then she squinted at me. "You actually should bleach your hair. I bet my friend would do it."

"Okay, sure," I said sarcastically.

"I'm serious. It would give you a few hours away from your kids."

"A few hours?!" I scooted away from her dramatically.

"Yeah, it takes a while to set." She looked at me. "You should do it. It would look so good. And if you hate it, just cut it."

"No, I gotta cover my earring." I said it like a joke, but I wasn't joking.

"Oh my gosh, you're fine." She looked at me as if I were in middle school, insecure about my looks. "I'd even pay for it."

"No," I told her.

"Again, it would be a few hours away from your kids," she told me.

"I don't hate them, Kelly," I said. I'd come to realize they weren't as crazy as I'd thought—they were about three times crazier, but they were fun, and cute, and worth it. Still, a few hours of sitting and doing nothing did sound nice.

"I know, but I want to see a blond Austin."

Curiosity overcame me, too. "Ya know what, what the heck?"

She lit up, making it all worth it.

"I'll text my friend to see when she can get you in."

*　*　*

I was blond the next day—as blond as my brown hair could get. The stylist made it so the roots would look okay when they'd grow out. Kelly's friend touched up the shagginess but kept my hair long enough to cover the earring. I made sure of it. She was married, and I realized I was paying attention to every new girl's ring finger as if I really thought anyone could take Cara's place.

10

AUSTIN

Mother's Day, Bella's birthday, and Kaleigha's birthdays were all within the same week of each other. Last year, Bella had been born on Mother's Day, which Cara had thought was fitting, amusing, and slightly annoying because once every six years or so, Bella's birthday and Mother's Day would land on the same day. She hadn't complained, but I felt bad that the one day she was supposed to be able to relax last year, she had to give birth.

When Mother's Day rolled around, I explained the event to Kaleigha and how Donna may be sad because she missed Cara.

"I'm sad, too, because I miss Mommy," Kaleigha told me.

"Me too, kiddo." I embraced her, misting up.

I invited Donna and Charlie out for lunch, because I felt like we needed to do something to celebrate.

When we met them at an Italian restaurant, Donna's favorite, we didn't really know what to talk about. A lump anchored itself in my throat. It had only been two months.

Kaleigha clung to me and refused to leave my lap at lunch. I liked her company because she didn't expect awkward small talk.

"Are you excited to hit the road again?" Donna asked.

I ripped up the bread, dipping it in the olive oil and parmesan cheese enhanced by pepper, and handed it to Kaleigha. "Try this," I told Kaleigha. Her little fingers took it from mine before she stuffed the food in her mouth. Then I told Donna, "I guess you could say that."

"What does that mean?"

"I mean, there's a bit of apprehension with everything."

"What are you apprehensive about?"

"More," Kaleigha said.

Ripping the bread for her again, I dunked it in the oil and handed it to her. "Careful. Keep it over the plate." I looked back at Donna, putting a hand on Kaleigha's bare shoulder beside the strap of her pink dress. "Leaving."

Kaleigha shifted on my lap, looking up at me. "You leaving?" she asked.

"Not for a long, long time," I said quietly.

"No," she said loudly. "You can't go! Mommy's gone—you can't go!"

Heat radiated from my face as I felt the stares of strangers. "Shhh. Shhh," I whispered. "I'll come back," I told her. "Don't worry."

"No, Daddy."

I would never yell at her for being worried about me leaving. Her mother had died. "Hey," I kissed her wavy brown hair. "I love you, and I'll always come home, okay? And Mommy loved you very much." My voice broke as I rested my chin on her head.

"Why's she gone?" Her tears started.

It was impossible to explain.

"Hey, Kaleigha," Charlie said, "do you wanna go on a walk?"

"Okay." Defeat broke through her tears. She scurried off of my lap.

Charlie stood and picked her up. They walked out. I couldn't take care of my own kid. *What is wrong with me?*

"I'm sorry," I told Donna.

Donna reached over to grab my hand. "You okay?"

"Today is not going to be an easy day." I couldn't look at her. I couldn't bear to see the tears in her eyes. My kids didn't have their mother, and Donna didn't have her daughter. And I just missed my wife. My chest ached.

Donna nodded. "It's not."

"I don't know if I want to bring them to the gravesite today."

"That's okay," she told me. "Have you been over there yet?"

Shaking my head, I attempted a weak smile. "I haven't."

"You can just say it's you who doesn't want to go."

I cringed. "I just don't know how Kaleigha will react."

"It might help to explain things."

"It might. Or it might confuse her more," I said. "I don't know."

She scrunched her eyebrows together. "How do you think you'd do with it?"

"I think I'd do okay." I cleared my throat. "Like, I know her body is there, but I know where she's really at, ya know?" Saying this out loud hadn't brought the certainty I'd hoped for.

Nodding, she wiped tears from her eyes. "Amen."

Despite how good bread submerged in olive oil, pepper, and parmesan cheese tasted, I was not hungry. When Charlie came back with Kaleigha, they were both giggling.

Because my mom's lasagna was one of my favorites, I got lasagna in honor of Mother's Day, but I couldn't stomach more than four or five bites. Maybe I was too busy debating whether I wanted to take the kids to the gravesite. I had no idea how it would affect Donna and Charlie or Kaleigha. I could control how I'd react unless they started getting emotional. If Charlie started crying, I'd probably start crying. I thought back to the visitation when I heard him sobbing and internally shuddered.

The waitress handed Charlie the check, and I tried to take it from him.

"Get your paws away, kiddo," he said, pulling it toward him.

"I invited you guys out," I told him.

"You're a mother to these kids, too, now," Donna told me.

For some reason, that really rubbed me the wrong way. I was nothing compared to Cara. And for my kids to know how amazing their mother was, I needed to keep her memory alive. Donna might be right; going to see Cara might help explain things—at least the logistics.

"We're going to see the place where Mommy's body is in the ground, but we won't see her," I explained to Kaleigha before we left.

"Why do you put her in the ground? That's mean."

There was a reason I'd explained it in front of Donna and Charlie: I figured they may be able to help.

"Because that's just what people do when someone passes away," Charlie told her. "We can't see her in Heaven with God, but she has a new body now."

"I want to see Mommy," Kaleigha said quietly, her eyes welling up.

Me too.

"Mama," Bella murmured.

So we went. We stared at a silver stone that said her name, date of birth, and date of death. I didn't feel anything. I knew she was dead, yet it didn't seem real. I was twenty-six years old and somehow a widower.

When we got home, Kaleigha and Bella went down for a nap, and I made my way to my favorite room of the house: my studio. Sure, I loved the master, but it was kind of lonely. I had two chairs in the nook of the bedroom, but it was only me in there now.

As I sat in the studio, I sat in front of the piano with a journal because I thought I could write. The fact I had met Cara in the first place seemed like the biggest blessing, but it meant losing her was even worse. And I didn't know if I was more pissed off that I'd lost her, that my kids wouldn't have her as their mother, or that Donna and Charlie had lost their child.

I started playing a random, slow melody on the piano that sounded a lot like something we'd written before, and I stared at my wedding ring. I didn't know why I still wore it. I thought about what our marriage meant. Literally, everything had revolved around me. The reason I'd been able to tour was because she was willing to stay home with the kids. She'd held off going on mission trips because of me until finally, we'd made it happen. She'd let me follow my dreams, so it was time for her to follow hers.

I'd gained an immense appreciation for her in the time she was away on the mission trip. I'd tried to tell her that all the time, too, while she was away and when she got back. I couldn't even complain about raising the girls on my own because she had been doing it since Kaleigha had been born.

If I had been home, would she still be here? She'd probably have a conniption if she knew I questioned that. But I shouldn't have taken the time with her for granted.

Then I thought about Kelly as I was fiddling around on the piano to try different piano parts for our song. I let my mind wander to what would happen if Kelly and Riley broke up—what would happen if I started dating her. How could I think such a thing? I stopped playing the piano, blinking back tears.

How could I think that after losing Cara?

I tore off my ring and chucked it across the room, telling myself I didn't even deserve to cry. Done with playing piano, I got up and grabbed the ring. I didn't want Bella to swallow it. I curled up on the bed in the studio, because that had been the guest bedroom replacement, too. It didn't seem right to put the ring back on as I played with it: a simple, silver ring.

I went down out of the studio and back up the other side of the upstairs. The staircase of our house was shaped like a "T" because the upstairs of our house was divided into two sections: a big room that had become my studio on one side, and on the other side, the three bedrooms. I walked into the master bedroom, into the closet where Cara's jewelry box sat on a shelf above her wedding dress and a few things Kelly and Donna had encouraged me to keep. Carefully, I took it down, sat on the floor, and opened the box. Her earrings, bracelets, and cross necklaces stared back at me.

Placing my ring in the box, I picked up her engagement ring and her wedding band with its little diamonds all around it. They were so small, just like her fingers.

The engagement ring's diamond was nearly a carat, an accomplishment I'd been proud of. I wished she were here to wear them again, and I wondered if Kaleigha and Bella would one day. Tears welled up in my eyes again, and even though I wasn't ready, I put the rings in her box, shutting it. Slamming the box on the shelf, I felt the overwhelming tightness in my throat.

Because we'd gone to a somewhat fancy restaurant, I was wearing black dress pants and a white button-down shirt. I decided to change into athletic shorts and a GreenButton crew neck, and I went back through the bathroom, fidgeting with my now vacant finger. When I made eye contact with myself, I noticed how much thinner I looked. I wished I could hold her hand, watching the rock still sparkle on her finger.

But I would never get to hold her hand again.

* * *

So many people had texted and called that day, simply just to check in. I didn't call anyone back because I was tied up with the girls, and I needed to call my mom after the girls were asleep. It took Kaleigha a little longer because of questions about Cara.

Mom asked me how I was.

"Okay," I told her.

"Just okay?" she asked.

Taking a deep breath, I paced the main floor of my new house that Mom and Dad hadn't seen yet. They were both too tied up with work to help me move. "Yeah."

"What does that mean?"

"It's been kind of a rough day."

"Do you want to talk about it?"

"No. Not really. How was your day?"

"Um—good, but I hate hearing you've had a rough day." She used the same type of tone I would use with Kaleigha whenever she was upset. "And you know if you ever need anything or need to talk, I'm always a phone call away."

I fought tears again, wishing they would just stop. Barely able to speak, I leaned on the fridge covered in Kaleigha's artwork. "Thanks," I somehow choked out.

"It's okay to have hard days."

Nodding, even though she couldn't see me, I took that truth in. I had forgotten that, because in the moment, it always seemed like the end. I took in another deep breath. "Yeah. What did you do today?"

She went on to tell me about how Luke, my oldest brother, took her to Hickory Park in Ames, and she told me about how she was done with classes for the semester. She asked me if I was considering going back to school.

"I mean, probably not. You know we just bought a house." *Or I, rather.*

"Is your label going to drop you?"

"No." Granted, the label didn't know I hadn't written much lately.

"You're still touring in the fall?" she asked me with her judgmental tone.

"Yes, that's the plan," I reminded her, annoyed. Somehow this conversation came up at least every other time we talked.

"It's not Donna and Charlie's job to watch your kids."

"It's also not your job to tell me what to do." I paused. "It's Mother's Day, and I called to tell you that you raised a son who can make his own decisions." I tried to defuse the seriousness.

"Yeah, that's the point. You're smart enough to know your kids need you, especially as their only parent."

"It's not like I want to be away, Mom." That was sort of untrue. I did want to go back on the road.

"It doesn't matter, Austin. They're going to think you don't care or don't want to be home with them."

"Mom, I can't do anything about it now." She had no idea the kind of day I'd had.

"You better not be planning on touring long-term. They need you."

"We'll see." Then I asked, "What would you do if I dyed my hair blond?"

"You wouldn't."

I didn't say anything.

"Why?" she asked after a moment.

"Kelly talked me into it."

"Your hair looked really light in Donna's Facebook photo, come to think of it."

"Yup."

"Do you want to get remarried?" she asked, joking.

Giving a chuckle, even though that subject stung a little, I told her, "Not right now."

But the question stung because I didn't know if I deserved another chance at marriage. I failed at taking care of my wife the first time.

11

SAM

Mother's Day was rough this year, like every other year. It had been nearly seven years since my parents had passed. With a rare leap of faith on this Sunday afternoon, my heart heavy thinking about Austin's kids and Cara's mom, I decided to call my older sister, Ali.

"Hey, what's up?" Ali answered, sounding kind of concerned.

"Hi, I was just calling because I was thinking about you." As the words came out of my mouth, I realized how stupid they sounded.

"Oh, I was thinking about you, too. How are you?"

"Fine." That was a lie, but whatever. I just wanted to talk to someone who understood. "How are you?"

"Okay."

"What are you up to?"

"Hanging out with Jon and his family," she told me. My dad's name had been John, and maybe that was why I didn't like her boyfriend.

"Oh, that's nice," I told her. "Tell his mom happy Mother's Day for me."

"Um, okay."

I didn't know what to say to that, forgetting why I'd called.

"What are you up to?" she then asked.

"Just hanging out."

"Are you on tour?"

"No."

"Because of Mother's Day?" She sounded genuinely curious.

"No, Austin's wife died suddenly in March, so we've been off the road."

"Oh, yeah, I guess that makes sense." Her lack of surprise told me she'd probably already heard about Cara.

"Yeah."

"How is he doing?"

"Uh . . ." I was standing on my balcony, and I couldn't remember the exact moment I'd come out here, barefoot, but I was leaning against the railing. "He's devastated, but he'll be okay." That was the most honest way I could express his pain.

"That's awful."

"Yeah, it is."

Ali was an English teacher, an adult, so I felt like I needed to act like one, too. I guess I was an adult, at twenty years old. It was weird living on my own, paying rent, working at a local coffee shop to pay the bills now that we were off the road . . . I was doing all the adult things, but she still seemed a lot older to me, even though she was only twenty-five.

"How are you doing?" she asked me, trying to be polite, not really asking.

"Okay. Mother's Day is always hard." I wasn't used to being so vulnerable.

"Yeah." Her voice lacked emotion.

"Yeah." My voice caught, again not knowing what to say. "When does school get out?"

"The end of May."

"That's coming up."

"Thank God."

"Is that why you wanted to be a teacher? To have summers off?"

"Yes. The only reason."

I tapped the railing with my fingers, imagining the wood as keys.

"Do you think you'll go back on tour?" she finally asked to fill the silence.

"I don't know. I think Austin wants to, but Chris and Tennyson don't really want to jump back on the road because their wives are kind of—everyone's pretty shaken up, but we make money doing shows, so there's that. Right now, I'm working as a barista instead."

"Oh, gotcha. Where are you working?"

"A local coffee shop called Blue Apron."

"Oh, cool."

"I'm also doing some coaching."

"Really?"

"Yeah. A girls soccer team here in Nashville. Middle schoolers."

"Do they all have crushes on you?" She sounded suddenly amused.

"Yeah, basically." It was funny to admit, but true.

"It's because your shaggy hair makes you look sixteen."

"Oh, shut up," I told her, rolling my eyes at the swimming pool I'd never used. No one ever did.

"Or because you're in a boy band." She had always made fun of me for being in a band, which was her job as my older sister.

"Sure."

"You seeing anyone?"

"Nope," I told her confidently.

"Oh . . ."

"How's Jon?"

"Good. Busy with work and stuff, but that's okay."

"At the shop still?" He worked as a mechanic or something.

"Yup."

"Cool. Tell him I say hi."

"Okay."

I had nothing left to say.

"Well, I better get back to the game we were playing, but thanks for calling." She'd found her cop out.

"Yup. Bye. Love you."

"Have a good day—or try to," she told me.

"You too."

"Bye."

Maybe I was overthinking it, but her not telling me she loved me back hurt a bit. I wondered if she really didn't. When I felt my eyes well up, I swallowed it back, trying to eliminate the tightness in my chest, but my whole body felt hollow. Why had I called her? That was so dumb. Gripping the railing, I reminded myself there was no point in grieving a relationship I didn't really have. I did miss my mom. I wanted to cry, but I refused.

When I came back, Aaron, my roommate, was watching TV in the condo. I wanted him to ask me how I was, but he didn't, so I just went to my room and played video games.

12

AUSTIN

Bella's birthday was the day after Mother's Day. Cara and I had once decided that even though Kaleigha and Bella's birthdays were so close together, we still wouldn't have their parties on the same day, but life happened. I told Kaleigha if we didn't have a dual birthday party, she would have to wait four extra days for presents. That wasn't a hard sell. I didn't tell her she would be getting more presents from me on her actual birthday because I didn't feel the need for her to anticipate it. She had enough to be anxious about.

Kelly came over to help decorate, hanging pink streamers all over the house. When Kaleigha and Bella woke up from their naps, they were pretty excited about the pink and mint green colors—Kelly's favorite colors. I wondered if Kelly liked mint green because her last name was Minty. Cara had liked mint green, but she'd especially enjoyed pale pinks and pastel colors even more so than Kelly.

We had the band, crew, and their families over, as well as Donna and Charlie. We grilled burgers and brats. Everyone brought something. It was the first time I'd hosted a party at our new house, but I needed it. They were my tight circle.

Kelly gave Bella a plastic Precious Moments toy of a blonde girl decorating a mint-green Christmas tree with pink tinsel. Very much a mixture of Kelly and Cara's favorite colors, and the toy sparked an odd moment of déjà vu.

Kaleigha kindly helped Bella open her presents. Kelly gave Kaleigha a squishy purse thingamajig, and Kaleigha would not put it down all night. I think she liked the feel of it. This was funny because other people gave her dolls and more expensive stuff, but all she paid any mind to was that cheap, memory-foam purse. Bella attached herself to her pink seal, a more silicone material. I think she liked the soft feel of it. It had just enough give to be satisfying to press on. Cara had given it to her last Christmas.

When Bella blew out a candle with the help of Kaleigha, I grew emotional, thinking about the reality that Cara wasn't there. If someone would've told her she wouldn't be able to watch her girls grow up, she would've been more than devastated.

Kelly and Donna helped me put the girls to bed, but Bella cried when we tried. I placed the pink seal and her new plastic toy beside her because it didn't have any pieces that would break off. Surprisingly, that calmed her down.

It was good to laugh and play games with my friends and family because the last few days had been draining. After everyone left, Kelly stayed to help me clean up.

"You okay?" she asked me.

"Yeah, yeah," I told her. "I just wish Cara was here to see this." I cleared my throat. "And she would've loved this house, even though it's lowkey a downgrade." I chuckled. "Not that that's what matters."

"You wouldn't have this house if it wasn't for her death." That was true, but I didn't understand her point.

"You're right. It doesn't have enough bedrooms for a family of six," I mumbled.

"What do you mean?" She raised her eyebrows.

"We had a five-bedroom house in hopes we'd have four kids," I told her. "At least, she wanted four kids." I paused. "I told her that we'd have as many kids as she wanted because I wasn't the one carrying them, so it wasn't my call." I took the trash out to the garage, not bothering to slip on shoes. Talking about dreams was a very intimate thing. Talking about shattered dreams was worse—way worse, actually.

When I came back up the stairs of the garage, Kelly greeted me with a hug. "That sucks."

Pulling away, I told her, "I'm lucky I have two girls." As I said the words, meaning it with every fiber of my being, the gratitude mixed with missing Cara overwhelmed me. I was so happy I had Kaleigha and Bella but so saddened Cara wouldn't get to be my partner in raising them; that's what she'd wanted more than anything.

"They're lucky to have you."

"I don't know about that."

"Cara did."

It didn't take long to clean up the house. "Do you wanna write?" I asked her, not wanting her to leave. I didn't want to be alone.

"Music?"

"Yeah."

She glanced at the time. It was getting late, but I didn't care. I didn't want her to leave, and I caught myself feeling that way. Was I just lonely, or did I want something more?

"Sure." She said it like she didn't care, but she followed me upstairs.

We wrote a brand-new chorus:

If there is a mustard seed of faith,
There must be hope
And if there is hope,
There is meaning
And this is just the beginning

When we were done, I gave her a hug. It was two in the morning when she finally left. I told her she could sleep in the spare bed in the studio, but she insisted she could make it home, because it really wasn't super late for her as she was still a touring musician. Two in the morning was late for me as I went to bed at ten now.

When I walked her to her car, we exchanged another embrace.

I wanted to kiss her, but I didn't. And I felt awful for even having that thought.

"Good night," she said before getting in the car and driving away.

When I felt sad to see her leave, I wondered why I enjoyed her company so much. Was it our connection through music? Was it our connection through losing Cara? Did I actually like her? What if I did like her? What kind of person would that make me?

~ 85 ~

13

RILEY

"I'm really thinking 'Bigger' will be a hit," Kelly explained on the way to the recording studio. I had picked her up. "I just feel it."

Running a hand through my ragged hair, I raised my eyebrows. "The demo alone gave me chills, so the actual thing is gonna kick ass."

"I haven't seen Austin that happy about something in a really long time," Kelly told me.

"That's good, I guess."

When we got to the studio, a now-blond Austin gave Kelly a hug, and she patted his back lightly.

"Are you blond now because blonds have more fun?" I snickered.

"Kelly convinced me," Austin said, bored.

"You said you were gonna do it!" Kelly exclaimed.

"I wasn't serious," Austin smiled, slapping his knee.

"Apparently you were," I mumbled. "I can see your earring, by the way." I pulled on his ear.

"Riley! Stop!" Austin scolded, grabbing my wrist and swinging my hand back even though I towered over him.

"You afraid you won't get to tour anymore if I rip it out?" I mocked.

He rolled his eyes, looking away, and I wondered if he legitimately thought keeping that dumb earring in determined whether or not we should still be a band.

"I wouldn't have to deal with you anymore." He folded his arms.

"You and I both know that's not true. I'll always be around."

"I hope we tour for a while," Austin said quietly, suddenly serious.

"I do, too." I put a light hand on his shoulder.

"I hope the other guys want to, too," he added.

"I know Sam does," I told him, "so that's majority, right?"

"Yeah." There was a distance in his voice.

"You think we will?" I asked him.

"I wish I knew for sure."

That was when Chris walked in.

"Hey," I said to him.

"What do you wanna know?" Chris asked us, being nosy.

"If we'll ever go back on the road long-term," I said bluntly.

Chris took in a deep breath, nodding. "Oh."

"Well, what do *you* think, Chris?" Austin asked.

Chris pressed his circular wired glasses against his nose. I hated how he tried to look hip, with his oversized off-white sweatshirt and gray skinny jeans. "I don't know. I mean, it's more up to you than us, man. We just play instruments sometimes decently."

Sam and Tennyson came by together, and when we got started with our favorite producer, Grayson Clay, we recorded the song. It took a couple of tries, because both Kelly and Austin forgot the lyrics, but when the final product came together, something happened as we played it back. Chris and Kelly cried, and Austin and Sam—well, they looked on the verge of tears, at least. Even with everything they'd both been through, I'd never seen either one of them actually shed a tear. I also wasn't much of a crier. Tennyson was the same way.

"This is so exciting," Austin exclaimed, giving Kelly a hug, and then giving the rest of us high fives. He was like a child who'd just won his first T-ball game.

14

SAM

One of the shows we decided to do was a summer festival in Iowa. For me, going to Iowa was always super weird because I never knew if I should tell Ali, but this time I did, and she told me I could stay with her at her townhouse.

It was funny because we took the tour bus down, and like normal, we left late enough that we slept through the ride. But when I woke up the next morning, there was a girl on the bus I'd never met before. She had long, curly brown hair—a very pretty girl, around my age.

"Hey," I said to her, blushing because she was cute and I had just woken up. I ran a hand through my thin, shaggy hair, hoping it wasn't obvious I'd just rolled out of bed.

"Hi," she said to me. The bus was stopped, but she still sat there, eating a bagel at the booth.

"Who are—what's your name?"

She said a name I couldn't pronounce, making me wonder if she was American.

"Sorry, one more time."

She tried again.

"Wait, Morgan?"

"No—" Still couldn't grasp it.

"Megan?"

"No." She giggled, rolling her eyes. "Just call me Mo."

"Like Missouri?"

She giggled. "Sure."

"Um, okay, Mo." I folded my arms, realizing I really had to pee. "What are you doing with us?" I tried to not sound accusatory, but why was this chick in our living space?

"Oh, I'm just here for the ride and to help out."

Blinking, I raised my eyebrows. "No, really, who are you?" She wouldn't tell me her name, and she was in our space. I had a weird feeling about this.

"I'm—!" Still didn't catch her name. "Don't worry, I'm supposed to be here."

"Where are you from, Mo?"

"A small town in Washington you've never heard of," she told me.

"Try me."

She did.

"Yeah, nope, never heard of it." I paused. "How did you end up on our bus?"

Nate came back in. "Imogen, do you want to run the lights tonight?" he asked her.

"Sure," she said.

Blinking a few times, I stared at her and then back at him.

"Wait, so are you crew?"

"Yeah!"

"Did you travel up with us?" Maybe she'd just gone straight to her bunk last night and I'd somehow missed her.

"Nope, I'm just going back with you guys." She was so excited, I could tell.

"Wait, do you live in Ames?"

Shaking her head, she told me, "Nope, I've just been volunteering at a camp near here."

"Which camp?"

She told me the name of the camp.

"My sister works there in the summer!" I exclaimed.

"Who's your sister?"

"Allison Lowe."

"Oh, Allison is the sweetest!"

I didn't know how to respond to that.

Mo added, "I interned there for half the summer, and now I'm going to do the other half of the internship touring with bands in Nashville for festivals."

"Oh, so you're just hitchhiking."

"Yes," she told me. "That's what it is."

"You're a spy, too, aren't ya?" Her face turned pink, and for some reason, my face turned pink, too. "Oh my gosh, you are!" I exclaimed, unable to stop thinking about how cute she looked.

"How did you know?" she asked me, playing along.

"It's . . ." I looked at her, enamored by her oversized gray shirt, the sleeves folded up, and her ripped jeans. But it was her hair that stood out the most. Her curly hair was gorgeous. I was convinced I was going to marry this girl. Something about her was different.

I noticed a tattoo of flowers on her forearm. "It's the tattoos. They're part of your cover."

"Oh, yeah. They're really easy to get off," she told me.

"The sarcasm is a part of your identity," I told her. "For the FBI."

"Well, sarcasm is my first language, so . . . that's why I got hired for the CIA, actually—get your facts straight."

"Dang, I was hoping you'd let me be your partner in crime." I smirked, hoping I didn't come across as too flirtatious.

I also really had to pee, but I felt like that would be weird now that a cute girl was on the bus.

"I don't even know *your* name," she told me.

"I'm Sam."

"Sam*uel*?" she asked.

"Oh, don't call me that."

"Why? Do you only get called that when you're in trouble?"

"I'm never in trouble, so I never get called that." *In other words, I'm never in trouble with my mom—who used to call me that—because she's dead.*

"Oh, so you're a goody two-shoes."

"He really is," Nate told her on his way out.

"I am not," I lied.

She curled her lips in.

I flashed a smile, hoping the church was unlocked because I had to pee very badly. I slipped past her.

"Okay, Samuel."

I also hated how my name rhymed with *mule*.

I asked Ali to come up to visit me in Ames because I didn't want to find a ride down to Ankeny. She picked me up from the church, and we landed at a cafe for lunch. Ali and I had nothing in common besides soccer, our last name, and our parents dying suddenly in a car accident.

"So, um, how's Austin?" she asked me when we sat in the booth.

"He's hanging in there."

"Yeah?"

Nodding, I tried to not think about Cara, because it was like I'd lost an actual sister.

"So, is this your only show for a while?"

"Yeah."

I didn't know what to talk to her about, so I just asked her about being a teacher to hold up the conversation. The waiter handed me the check, probably because I was the guy, despite the fact we looked like siblings. But whatever. I paid for lunch, even though she definitely made more money than me.

Luckily, I had to get back to the church for sound check, so Ali drove me there in silence.

When I made it to sound check, Ali told Austin she was praying for him, and that if he needed anything, she was there for him. I could only assume she was being genuine—it was hard to tell, because I didn't really know the real her. It wasn't like I thought she was a bad person; we just lacked the ability to click.

The show happened. It was weird because it was normal. I had to keep reminding myself that performing wasn't normal anymore, thankful for every moment we got on stage. Austin seemed to do okay. I'd been wondering if he'd get choked up, but he didn't.

I ended up staying on the bus with the rest of the crew instead of staying with Ali down in Ankeny. I told her I didn't want her to have to drive me back up for church the next day. Without the roll of the bus, I found it hard to sleep, and honestly, I wasn't in the best headspace, so I went out to the main cabin of the bus at around one in the morning, knowing no one would be out there. To my surprise, Mo was sitting at the booth, writing something down, and it freaked me out to see someone else awake.

"Oh my gosh," I whispered, putting my hand on my chest.

"What are you doing up?" she whispered.

"I couldn't sleep. You?"

"Same." She squinted. "You're not from Iowa?"

"No—well, sort of—my sister lives here, and I lived here for a while."

She nodded. "Where are you from originally?"

"Victoria, Texas."

"Never heard of it."

Shrugging, I said, "It's in southern Texas."

"Are your parents still there?"

I winced. "Technically, yes."

"Technically?"

"They're both deceased."

"Oh." She looked at me. "I'm sorry."

I stuffed my hands in my athletic shorts, not prepared to talk about it.

"How did it happen?" Then she added, "If you don't mind me asking."

"They both were killed in a car accident."

"Damn," she said. "That sucks. How long ago?"

A dim light flickered above the couch she was sitting on.

"About seven years ago." The seven-year anniversary was approaching, meaning I was expected to be over it by now, right? I wished that were the case.

"Wait, how old are you?"

"Twenty."

"You were thirteen?" she asked softly, just above a whisper.

"Yeah." Maybe it was because it was late and I was tired, but I felt a lump creep into my throat.

"That's . . . I'm sorry. Is it hard seeing your friends hang out with their parents?"

Keeping my distance intentionally to avoid revealing the tears in my eyes, I debated whether to lie or not. "I mean, I'm thankful that they have their parents, ya know?" I attempted a chuckle.

She just stared at me. "Are you close with your sister?"

"Not really," I admitted as my voice caught.

"That's why you came back to the bus," she realized.

Nodding, I pressed my lips together, hoping we were far enough away from each other that she wouldn't notice.

"Can I give you a hug?" she asked me.

It would be rude to say no, so I just nodded, looking down, trying to breathe evenly. When she pulled away, I couldn't even look at her as my face twitched, and so I covered it with both of my hands. She wrapped another arm around me, squeezing my shoulder.

"I'm just tired," I told her.

"It's okay to cry," she told me genuinely.

Rolling my eyes, I forced back the tears, shaking my head. "I don't want to cry," I told her. "It's not a big deal."

She raised her eyebrows. "Losing your family isn't a big deal?"

Shrugging, I admitted in a whisper, "I don't want to be—like, I'm not usually like this."

"I won't judge you." She paused. "Do you want space?"

Nodding, I took in a deep breath and walked back into my bunk. I attempted to push the negative thoughts away by thinking about how lucky I was to be in GreenButton, even though at that moment, I was more like an outcast without a family.

When I woke up the next morning, Mo was sitting in the booth again.

"How are you not asleep?" I asked her, pressing up my glasses.

"I could ask the same for you. How are you?"

I shrugged. I hadn't forgotten about the wee hours of the morning. Maybe it weighed me down because I refused to let it out the night before. I wasn't about to break down in the bus though. If I were ever going to break down, it would be alone. "I'm—I was just tired last night," I told her.

"You don't have to play it off like that," she told me.

My eyes immediately welled up again. I didn't want to be some dramatic kid defined by the fact he lost his parents.

I went into the pathetically tiny bathroom to pee. In the mirror, my eyes looked back at me, red and watery. I took in a deep breath and asked God silently, *Make it go away. Make it hurt less.*

And He said, *"Sit in it."*

I told Him, *I'm not gonna cry for this.*

We led worship at church that morning, and I ended up showing Mo and the rest of the crew around Ames. We went to the mall where she convinced me to buy a rainbow unicorn phone case, an aqua fox case, and a green dinosaur case. That day, Mo took my mind off of things, like Ali not wanting to hang out with me. Mo made me laugh a lot, and I didn't feel like she was judging me for being a mess.

15

AUSTIN

"I miss you, Daddy," Kaleigha said to me over FaceTime. She was sitting with Bella in Donna's lap.

"I miss you, too." I sat at the kitchen table of my parents' house.

Bella was holding her pink seal and the Christmas ornament toy Kelly had given her. "Dadda!" She tried touching me through the screen.

"Hey, Bella!"

"Dadda!" She tried to take the phone from Donna, but Donna kept the phone steady. Bella burst into tears.

"She misses you," Donna told me.

"I miss her, too." My voice gave out.

Mom walked over, squeezing my shoulder.

"Y'all wanna say hi to Grandma Brooklyn?"

Close enough that I could feel her coffee breath, Mom leaned over my shoulder. "Hey, Kaleigha and Bella!"

Kaleigha waved.

"Bella, can you say hi?"

"Hi." Her voice softened. Then she reached for the phone and shrieked, "Dadda!"

"I'll see you tomorrow," I promised, reminded that every time I'd left Cara, Kaleigha, and Bella, I missed them before I even said goodbye. "Kaleigha, can you tell Grandma and I what you did with Nana, Papa, and Bella?"

"Church, and we got—we got . . ." She looked up at Donna. Donna waited, letting her work out her thoughts on her own. "Pink mac 'n' cheese!"

"Pink mac 'n' cheese?!" Mom and I both exclaimed as if oddly colored food was the most exciting thing ever.

"And color."

"You colored?" I asked.

"Yeah."

"Can I see?"

Kaleigha looked up at Donna. "Go ahead," Donna told her. "I think it's still on the table."

Kaleigha hopped off Donna, and then Donna asked, "How was your show last night?"

"Good." I glanced back at my mom.

"How are you doing, Donna?" Mom asked.

"All right. How are y'all?"

"Good."

"When does school start up again?" Donna asked.

"Late August."

Kaleigha scampered back into view with a pink scribbling over a coloring book page of a princess I didn't recognize. "Wow, good job, Kaleigha!" I exclaimed.

"That's really good!" Mom said. "Do you wanna see Grandpa Brooklyn?"

"No," Kaleigha said passively.

"Kaleigha," I said over the screen in a disapproving tone. "You don't want to see your grandpa?"

"Fine." I pictured her as a teenager and shuddered before burying that thought.

"Dad!" I yelled from the dining room table.

"Austin!" he yelled back, being a smart aleck.

"Wanna say hi to Kaleigha and Bella?"

"Sure." Dad walked in behind Mom and me. He waved at them. "Hi!"

"It's Grandpa Brooklyn!" I announced, still not used to saying that.

"Hi!" Kaleigha said.

Bella said "Dadda" again.

"Seems like she misses you," Dad told me, patting me on the back.

Then Kaleigha showed him the picture, but her attention was swept away by her little sister's desire to wander around the living room, so Kaleigha started playing house with her tiny baby doll that she'd named Bella. Kaleigha was usually a little more creative with names.

*　　*　　*

"I cannot believe you're going back on tour this fall," Mom told me a little while later as we were outside, enjoying the humidity of Iowa . . . said no one ever. The clouds mixed with the dense air.

I frowned at her for bringing it up.

"How long do you think you'll tour for?" she pressed again.

"As long as we can."

"Austin," Mom said quietly, "what about the girls?"

"They're in good hands."

"I know, but it's not Donna and Charlie's responsibility to watch them." Mom glanced over at Dad, trying to gain his support.

Dad sipped his beer.

"They offered, though," I reminded her.

"So, if you were divorced and had a different job, and your wife offered to take the kids two-thirds of the time, would you be okay with that, or would you fight for at least fifty-fifty custody?"

"This is different." I put a hand up, taking a sip of my beer. I couldn't remember the last time I'd had a beer. I'd sort of missed it.

"You're right," Mom said, attempting an impartial tone. "You're their only living parent, and you want to be gone the majority of the time. Luke fought for fifty-fifty custody of his kids."

Luke, my oldest brother, had two kids with two different women. He also owned a sports bar in downtown Des Moines. He had a solid beard and drove a motorcycle: badass. Not a failure, but never went to college, so he was never enough for Mom. Neither was I.

Taking another sip of beer—now because I needed it—I didn't try to mask my fallen face. "I know it's not ideal."

"You're choosing the band over your kids."

Mom and Dad, but mostly Mom, had never been a fan of me being on the road while having a family, but she'd gotten over it when we did it anyway. And then Cara died.

Looking her dead in the eyes, I said, "I am not!"

"Actions speak louder than words, Austin," Mom told me. "You've always chosen the band over your family, and that was fine while you were single, but now it's time to grow up and settle down. You need to get a job where you're home every night because Nana and Papa's schedule shouldn't revolve around you."

"For the last time, they offered," I snapped.

"Yeah, and shame on you for taking advantage of them!" she yelled.

"Brenda," Dad warned.

Getting up from the Adirondack chair, snatching the beer, I started for the sliding door, turning back as I slid it. "You're just jealous that you're hardly involved in their lives," I yelled, tears welling up in my eyes.

"Oh, so you wanna get on me for not being in their lives?" she cackled eerily. "You're the primary caregiver who wants to be gone two-thirds of the time. Cara gave up everything for those kids, and she died when you were away, and you want to leave every weekend as if nothing happened!"

Dad tried to de-escalate both of us, but neither one of us paid attention to what he was saying.

"It's not that easy to just quit, Mom." I struggled to slide the door closed.

"That's a cop out!"

When I finally got in the kitchen, I slammed my beer on the counter. Spike, their dog, barked at me, but what startled me was the tear rolling down my cheek. Wiping it quickly, I felt another tear slip, too. I made my way to the bathroom where I could lock myself in, neglecting Spike.

I leaned against the cupboards, covering my face, surprised how quickly the tears came. I caught sight of the stranger in the mirror as I wiped my cheeks more thoroughly. *I don't even know you.*

Why did this, of all things, make me so upset?

They could never know.

In the bedroom I'd grown up in, I attempted to tune the dusty guitar that had never made it to Nashville. I restrung it with neon-green plastic strings my grandma had given me in high school. I knew they'd be awful quality, so I'd never wasted my time putting them on any guitar, but I wanted to see how bad they really were.

16

RILEY

Cara had once concocted a whole plan to lure Kelly into getting her nails done when I was ready to propose. That wasn't going to happen now, but I texted Charlie, asking him if he'd be willing to chat.

He invited me over for a beer on a warm Sunday evening, and we landed in Charlie and Donna's sunroom. We talked about guns for a little while. He told me about all the guns he owned. Sharing what little information I knew about guns, I just pretended to agree with all his stances on the Second Amendment, because I didn't really know what I really thought, and I didn't really care. All I knew was that I personally did not need to own a gun.

"Do you wanna know why I'm here?" I finally asked, taking in the white tile, the perfect all-American home.

"You wanna marry my daughter."

I leaned back in my chair, inhaling and exhaling a slow breath, finding myself beaming. "Yeah, I do."

"Well, the last time I let my daughter marry a GreenButton member, she died." He took a sip of his beer.

I picked a callus at the tip of my finger. "Please don't ever say that to Austin." My voice was sterner than I'd anticipated for a conversation about marrying his daughter.

"I didn't mean it like that." He put his hands up. "It was a joke, Riley." Not wanting to say the wrong thing to my future father-in-law, especially given his circumstances, I just looked at him. "Yes, you can marry Kelly." He sat up straight. "As long as you treat her as well as Austin treated Cara. He set pretty high standards." I didn't know if he was joking or trying to intimidate me. Maybe a mixture of both?

Nodding, I said, "Well, Cara deserved the world, and so does Kelly."

"I know." Then he paused. "You remember I own a few guns though, right, kiddo?"

"You mentioned something about that."

We transitioned to football.

As I walked out of the sunroom, Donna was watching TV.

"Hey," I said to Donna. "There's something I want to talk to you about."

"Yeah?" She raised her eyebrows.

Looking at Donna's hands, noticing her perfect maroon nails, I sat on the couch in the other corner, facing her. "Cara was going to help me find the perfect ring for Kelly." My voice broke— *dammit.* "And Cara was going to trick Kelly into getting her nails done when the time came to propose." Talking through it restored my voice.

Donna's blue eyes welled up. "I know, sweetie. Cara told me."

"I was wondering if you'd help me." I was crying, I realized, feeling the warm tears run down my cheeks. It was strange, because I didn't really cry when Cara had passed. I had teared up maybe three times.

"Of course, sweetheart."

I wiped my face with both of my hands. "I'm sorry," I said. "I just feel for you and Kelly and Charlie—and everyone."

"It's okay, darling," Donna whispered in her thick southern accent, pulling me into a hug. When I pulled away, she cupped my face, wiping my tears with her thumbs. Even though these people would be my second parents, I wasn't super comfortable with her touching my face, despite how sweet it was.

"What did you say to him?" Charlie asked Donna, walking past us.

"I told him he can't marry Kelly."

"Oh, good. I told him the same thing." Charlie winked at me, nudging my back with the knuckles of his fist.

"I'm sorry," I said, wiping my eyes again.

"You're fine." Charlie squeezed my shoulder.

"When do you think you'll propose?" Donna asked, changing the subject.

"I don't know yet. Whenever I have a ring and her nails are done. I know what I'm gonna do. I'm gonna do it during a show." I sniffed, trying to avoid a runny nose.

"Because you're going on tour together?" Charlie asked me.

"Yeah."

"I'd . . . be careful with that," Donna said.

My heart sank. "Do you think she'd say no?"

"No, she'll say yes." She gave me a weak smile, wiping tears from underneath her eyes. "It just might sting a little for Austin."

"He'll be fine," Charlie said.

"Do you think it would be better to do something more intimate?"

"We don't wanna hear about your sex life," Charlie told me.

"Oh, my gosh." I rolled my eyes, feeling my cheeks go red. "How much beer did you have?"

"Not enough to have you as an in-law," Charlie told me.

"Were you like this with Austin?"

"Nope." Charlie slammed my back. "Austin's ego wouldn't be able to handle it."

"Charlie," Donna warned.

"What did you do when Austin asked if he could marry Cara?"

"I cleaned my guns in front of him."

"You did not!" Donna called out.

"No, I think he asked me at Thanksgiving in 2009, and then he proposed on her birthday two days later. He already had the ring and everything." He was teary all of a sudden.

"I remember that," I said.

They both nodded.

Filling the silence, I asked, "Can I ask you guys a question?"

"You just did," Charlie told me. "You only get one."

Rolling my eyes, I asked anyway, "How do you guys feel about Austin still touring?"

Donna and Charlie exchanged glances.

"We're happy to help in any way that supports y'all," Donna said, "and it means we get to spend time with the girls, so it works out. I do know it's hard for Austin to be away, though."

Charlie nodded.

"How do you guys stay so positive?" I asked them.

"We know where she's at," Donna told me.

17

TENNYSON

"How much longer are y'all gonna be on the road?" Elena and I were sitting on the couch after Joshua went to bed.

"I don't know."

Her hair was down, and she ran a hand through her thin blonde, almost-white hair, sighing.

"Sorry," I told her.

"I just—I know you don't know, but Mom and Dad don't love watching Joshua every time I have a shift and you're gone."

"I know. I know."

"What if you just finished out this tour and called it?" She looked at me.

"You want me to quit." I clenched my jaw.

"I do. I want my husband home. And I make enough that you would have some flexibility about what you wanted to do."

I looked around at our small living room, staring out the window. "I don't know if I'm ready for that—to just be done in a few months."

"There's never going to be a good time, Tennyson."

Staring at the black silicone band around my finger, I said, "I know, but you're asking me to leave them without a drummer."

"You said they'd find a replacement."

*　*　*

I called Keaton, our first piano player. He reminded me how he'd quit the band and the band had survived.

*　*　*

Austin asked me to come over after I'd texted him that I wanted to chat because he didn't want to find a babysitter. I knocked on the door—hopefully his kids were asleep. He had left the light on for me.

"Hey," he greeted quietly, clasping my hand, then tapping my chest with his.

"Hi." I slid off my tennis shoes.

"How are things?" he asked me, leading me into the living room. He was wearing black sweatpants and a V-neck shirt.

"Good." I gave an automatic response. "How are you?" I sat down in the chair closest to him, next to the windows.

"I'm okay," he told me, nodding.

"What did you do today?"

"I . . ." He offered me a smile, letting out a laugh. "I let Kaleigha pretend to do my makeup, and I wrote half a song. You?"

"I did not let Joshua do my makeup."

"Really? I thought that would be something he'd be into, especially at his age."

"Nope."

He smirked, acting amused for a second, and then he asked, "So, what's going on?"

I did my best to say what I needed to without letting out word vomit: "I care a lot about you, and Chris, and Riley, and Sam, and Nate—everyone in the crew, but—I love touring, I just—Elena wants me to stop touring, and I guess that ultimately means I would have to leave the band."

He wasn't looking at me anymore as he stared at the blank TV, nodding slowly. "Okay," was all he said.

"Okay, what?" I asked after a second.

"I just—I just didn't expect that." He managed a smile for me, but pain overtook his eyes.

"I'm sorry."

"No, you know what you need. Are you and Elena doing okay?"

When I didn't know how to answer such a simple question, I looked away. My vision started blurring.

He didn't say anything as he waited. I felt his eyes on me as I admitted, "I don't know."

"You don't know?"

"I . . . I think so, but I don't know."

"Are you . . . like, have you been thinking about this for a while?"

"Yeah. It's hard with her being a nurse and the weird hours. Elena works a lot of weekends, shifts that daycare doesn't always cover, so she has to ask her parents for a lot of help, and . . . anyway, she said I can work until we find a replacement."

Austin just nodded, taking my words in.

"I'm sorry," I repeated.

"Don't be." He sounded like Austin before Cara had died: clear and compassionate, not blank. Then he asked, "So, how *are* you guys doing?"

"I mean, we're fine, but it's just—it's been a really tough six months."

"How is Elena doing with everything?" Austin—kind enough to ask about Elena when he was the one widowered.

"She's . . . I mean, she has a lot going on, especially with her job."

"Why now, though?" he asked genuinely.

"It's been a really hard six months." My voice caught on my words, so I paused for a second. "And I know it's even tougher on you, but I just think it would be better if I was home."

He didn't say anything. He looked sad. Defeated.

"Are you mad?" I asked quietly, almost needing him to say he wasn't and that the band would be okay.

"No?" He didn't sound convincing. "It's just . . ." He bit his lip, shaking his head. "I get it. And a part of me wonders if we should be touring in the first place, anyway."

"Honestly, we shouldn't be," I told him bluntly.

"Like we have a choice," he scoffed.

"We do."

"I don't know what else I would do."

"Be home with your kids." I said it with a little more aggression than I had intended.

"I don't even know what I'd wanna do."

"You could be a worship pastor."

"Yeah, maybe." His voice sounded distant again. "When are you planning on leaving the band?"

"When we find a replacement."

Austin stared at the blank TV, resting his elbow on the armrest.

"Are you okay?" I asked him.

"Yeah." He looked down. "I'm just thinking."

"'Bout what?"

"Whether we should do this anymore." He put a hand through his hair, clenching his jaw.

"You know you don't have to be in GreenButton forever."

I could hear his voice shake a little. "What are you going to do?"

"Don't know. Get a job." I paused. "What are you passionate about?"

"Music. Jesus. People."

Which was why he was so good at his current job.

"Great. What can you do with that?"

"I don't know." His voice wavered. "I'm doing it right now, but . . ."

I waited, but he didn't say anything. Something was just off. Really off.

"But what?" I normally wouldn't pry, but his distance . . . I felt a responsibility to make sure he was okay.

"I feel so bad being away from my kids after everything." Any attempt to steady his voice failed him. "And I respect you for wanting to take a step back, and I think it's just a lot to take in because I might have to follow in your footsteps."

"Touring is hard when you're married. I can't imagine how hard it is when you're a single parent and grieving." This was the most serious conversation I'd ever had with him.

He twisted his earring. A part of me wanted to rip it out of his ear for him. Then he rubbed his nose with his finger while gripping his chin with his thumb. "Should we keep doing this?" The smallness in my best friend's voice reminded me none of this was easy for him. For a while, we'd kind of just pretended like nothing had happened.

"Do you really wanna know what I think?"

"Yeah."

I had to be careful. I didn't want to crush him. "You think there are no other options besides touring, but if you really didn't want to tour, you'd figure out a way not to."

"What are my options, Tennyson?"

"How long do you want to be in the band?"

"I don't know anymore." He stared at his sweatpants, his hair falling over his forehead. Then he said, "I don't know how to replace you when we don't even know how much longer we can do this."

"I'm sorry to put this on you." I put a hand on his shoulder.

"Don't be. You're just doing what's best for your family."

18

AUSTIN

"This next award is for the best single of the year." Hannah from Resin Ring stood next to her sister, both in purple dresses with their hair pulled up in curly buns. "Sometimes an artist can feel when a song is going to be special. The nominees are . . ." The video played, announcing all the nominees, including our song. Even though we knew we'd been nominated, I thought I would've felt some sort of anxiety or pride, but I didn't really feel anything.

The last time we'd been nominated and won New Artist of the Year, we were all in awe. The other artists were very good, but a part of me had thought maybe we had a chance. The other artists who'd been nominated were our friends, or at the very least, acquaintances, and they were extremely talented. When we won, I had forgotten everything I'd planned out as an acceptance speech, spurting out words of gratitude. That was probably the most emotional anyone had ever seen me—even Cara.

"And the best song of the year goes to 'Let Me Trust You' by GreenButton."

Oh, shoot, now I have to talk. Yay.

I hugged everyone I knew until we got up to the stage. The thought of hugging Cara crossed my mind, but she wasn't there, I remembered, as I shook hands with the people who didn't win. If I had been voting, I would've voted for "Let Me Trust You," but I was extremely biased, and I knew the others were talented, too.

When all of us got up on the stage, I hugged Hannah and Valerie. Chris took the shiny trophy. I looked into the lit-up crowd, standing in front of the podium. Hundreds clapped as I exchanged glances with Chris. He put his hand on my shoulder.

"Um." I sounded out of breath. "Thank you." My eyes were drawn to where Megan and Elena were sitting, and for a split second, I expected to see Cara clapping alongside them. "What most people don't know is, I wrote this song on the bus at like two in the morning on the night of the Sandy Hook shooting, and we had considered canceling the show that evening, and when I asked my late wife—" My voice caught because I'd never used that term. "—she told me we still needed to do the show, because that's what people needed after a day like that. She reminded me that sometimes your prayer needs to be, 'God, let me trust You.'"

As I heard my words, I didn't believe them. I started to go through the routine people to thank, starting with Cara. "Of course, I have to thank Cara, my wife. Her parents, Donna and Charlie, for raising such an amazing daughter. Everyone in the band: Chris, Riley, Tennyson, Sam. Our crew. Our manager, Nate. Our label. But most importantly, God, and the gift of faith

He provides to the brokenhearted." Out of breath, I stepped back from the mic.

Chris kept an arm around me as I barely heard the applause. We had won Christian music in a way, but I didn't feel anything. Donna embraced me. Megan embraced Chris. Charlie was Kelly's plus-one because Riley was invited with GreenButton. Donna was my plus-one because I knew both Donna and Charlie wanted to come for Kelly, and honestly, they genuinely wanted to be there for me, too.

I wanted Cara, and I wanted to cry, but not here.

The rest of the show seemed to go on forever. At least the trophy was shiny to look at.

When I got home, I called my parents like I'd promised my mom I would.

"Congratulations!" Dad told me, answering Mom's phone.

"Y'all already know?" I asked.

"We have our ways of finding out," Mom told me.

They must've been on speaker. "Who? Donna?"

"We'll never tell," Mom told me.

"Why did I need to call you then?"

"Because we are so proud of you," Mom said.

"Now, where are you going to store another big trophy?" Dad asked.

"Next to the other one." I totally had a plan just in case we'd won.

"How are you feeling as a two-time winner?" Mom asked me.

Speaking weakly, I admitted, "I wish Cara had been there." I wanted them to say something that would make it better.

"She was there in spirit," Mom said quietly. "And she would be so proud of you."

That didn't help, but Mom was right. Cara would be proud. Which only made it worse.

When I finished talking, I went into the studio to let myself cry. But nothing came. I was supposed to be happy. I was also supposed to be sad. I was supposed to feel something, but I felt nothing other than heaviness.

19

RILEY

Walking up onto the stage with the mic, nerves pulsated through me. I wasn't a good singer in general, and I definitely wasn't a good singer when I was nervous, but Kelly loved it when I sang anyway.

I was supposed to come in while she was singing one of her songs. As soon as she was done, her keys player, Embry, would start the song I would be singing, and Kelly's mic would be turned off.

That was not how it went at all.

I came onto the stage, singing, sure, but my mic was not working. Kelly looked back at her band members, confused. Although she didn't jump, I could tell I'd startled her. I kept on singing, hoping the crew would turn on the damn mic. But they didn't, so I just went for it. I got down on one knee, still singing the song I'd prepared as I pulled the box out of my pocket, flipping it open with one hand (I had practiced). Looking up at her, I asked, "Will you marry me?" into the mic, which it finally picked up.

She covered her mouth with both of her hands, her nails a blinding bright pink. With the glistening lights, I couldn't tell if there were tears in her eyes or not. Her strategically loose ponytail bounced as she nodded her head intensely. "Yes, yes, yes!" My mic picked up her excitement as the crowd freaked out. She knelt down to kiss me, grabbing my cheeks, her soft lips meeting mine.

When she pulled away, I placed the ring on her finger, thankful it fit.

"Y'all!" she yelled into her mic, staring at the ring, leaning on me. "This ring is stunning!" The deep-red stone glimmered on her finger, surrounded by little diamonds. Cara had mentioned Kelly would probably want something red, something classic. But I couldn't remember anything else Cara had said. When trying to figure out Kelly's ring size, there had even been a moment where I'd thought to myself, *We could just ask Cara.* Nope. We couldn't. Cara had known the right size, but I wasn't sure if she'd ever told me or not. Donna and I ended up guessing.

It was a beautiful moment, but when I glanced backstage, I saw Austin peering onto the stage. His face was blank, but when our eyes met, he gave me a toothless smile.

20

AUSTIN

I walked into the conference room, pulling out my phone. I landed on social media, and Riley and Kelly's engagement blew up the band's notifications. Strangers were saying things like:

Congrats Kelly and Riley!
They're such a cute couple!!!
So fun to see this couple get engaged!
There was a beautiful ring to the music tonight!
They are so sweet!

People posting about a couple they didn't even know getting engaged reminded me Kelly Minty was more famous than us, but I legitimately found it kind of creepy. It also pissed me off. The whole thing infuriated me because I wanted to be happy for them—I *did*. And I was, I guess. But I just didn't want to see it or think about it. Still, I did my best to acknowledge the mentions and tags as they piled in.

Somehow, I landed on Cara's Instagram page. There she was, alive again, her curly natural-blonde hair standing out amongst the rest of her. She held Bella right after she'd been born. Even when visibly worn out—understandably, after giving birth—she was still so beautiful. I missed her aquamarine eyes the photo failed to capture. How does someone in their twenties go from one hundred to zero so quickly from a disease that mirrored a cold? How? Why?

I was mad at myself for even scrolling through photos of her. But I wanted to see her. I wanted to feel her. Remember her. See her. Smell her hair. See the color of her eyes. Be with her. But if she walked into this room at that very moment, she wouldn't even recognize me after everything I'd been through. The thought of her knowing how the loss had affected us made me cringe, because she'd be devastated to know how hard this was. I wondered if she'd known she was going to die. I didn't think so, because she would've done everything in her power to get help.

It didn't make sense. It literally didn't make sense. God was faithful; she went on a mission trip to share the hope of the gospel. And now we were living the hope of the gospel—or supposed to be. It was like there was this pressure to trust God now more than ever, but there was a part of me that didn't know if I even believed it. If God were truly faithful, why wouldn't He show His faithfulness by letting her live? Or if He really was faithful by letting her go home early, what was the point of anything on this Earth? I didn't get it.

When the door opened, I reflexively locked my phone, putting it flat on the table, facing up. It was Chris.

"Whatcha up to?" He came over, the door closing behind him.

"Just chillin'." I looked up at him. "Are people loading up?"

"Yeah." He towered over me, perhaps debating whether to sit or not.

"Okay." Sighing, I knew I had to get up and help out, but I was glued to the chair.

"How are you doing?"

I picked up my phone again, tapping the green button, not even knowing why. I thought about telling him, but I didn't want to talk. "I'm tired."

"Why are you tired?"

"I dunno. It's late." I clicked the green button again to check the time: it was 11:23 p.m.

"It's not that late." A hint of attitude leaked into his voice. "But how are you doing with the whole Riley and Kelly thing?"

"I'm happy for them." I stared at the gray speckled table that was too similar to Chris's crew neck.

"Yeah?"

"Sure." I pointed my palms up to the ceiling, shrugging.

He didn't say anything.

"What?" I demanded.

"I didn't say anything." He put his hands up.

"But you're thinking something," I told him.

"Yeah, I was standing right next to you as we watched Riley propose, and I saw your face."

"Your point?" I didn't look at him as I heard the unintentional coolness in my voice.

"That is my point, Austin."

My eyes started welling up. "I want to be happy for them, Chris, I do," I spat out.

"But?" His voice was quiet.

"I—this is stupid. I should be happy for them." My voice grew louder, but my throat was tight. "Kelly's been through hell, too, and this is a really good thing for her, so . . ." I groaned, blinking back tears, frustrated that I couldn't even find the words. Even if I could formulate a full sentence, my throat was suddenly suffocating my speech.

"So, what?" he asked.

"So, I shouldn't be mad!" My voice cracked. "This is so stupid."

"What's stupid?"

"That this is affecting me." I covered my face when tears splattered onto my cheeks.

"Why is it stupid?" He placed a light hand on my back, and his voice was kind.

"Because . . . they're happy." I sounded small.

"I can see how this would sting," he said, barely above a whisper.

"I don't want them to walk in here and then feel bad about it." I wiped my cheeks with my fingers before hiding my face in my hands again.

"Don't worry about them. They're doing their own thing right now."

I didn't say anything.

Then I heard the door open behind us and Nate's voice. "Y'all wanna help load?"

Lifting my head, I saw Nate in the doorway. "Yeah." I faked enthusiasm as my voice cracked.

"Are you okay?"

I didn't respond as I looked down.

"Austin?" he pushed, more compassionately.

"Let's go load." I got up with my head down, starting to walk out.

Nate stopped me by grabbing my shoulder. "Hey."

"What?" I asked, continuing down the hall.

"Why don't you just—you wanna talk?"

"Talk about what?"

"Why you're—what's wrong?"

"It's fine," I mumbled.

"Do you—why don't you and Chris relax?"

"Nope." I said sternly, wiping my nose, continuing.

"You might wanna go the other way," Nate called.

Doing a one-eighty, I went back the other way, storming through the hall. I wanted to punch something. Or someone.

21

TENNYSON

"Hey!" I answered Keaton's phone call.

"What's up, man?" he asked.

"Not a whole lot. How are you?"

"Busy, but good. You?"

"Okay," I said.

"How's tour?"

"It's tour." Then I asked, "How's your internship going?"

"Um . . ." He let out a soft laugh. "It's fine."

"What does that mean?"

"It means . . ." He sighed. "It means that people are broken, so churches are filled with broken people. So it's fine."

"Did something happen?"

"Um, yeah, but it's fine."

"Okay. Well, what happened?"

"They're just—they are people and people sometimes do hurtful things. Say hurtful things."

"To you? Or other people?"

"Me."

"What did they say about you?"

"They found out about Marah."

"Mhmm. What happened between you two anyway?"

"She—it's kind of a long story."

"I have time."

"You would never—you would literally never look at me the same way again."

"Bet. Unless you murdered someone."

It took longer than a second for him to say, "So, that's the thing . . ."

"Wait, what?" My heart fell into my chest. I didn't want to have to report my friend.

"I mean, everything was legal."

"What does that mean?"

"So, when I was at Iowa, I got a girl pregnant at a party and paid for an abortion, and I didn't tell Marah because I hadn't told anyone. One day, somehow the topic of abortion came up, and I told my mentor—a guy who I trusted dearly—the truth, and he didn't seem to make a huge deal out of it. But a few weeks later, I got called into the dean's office. They told me I was no longer welcome to study at the seminary, so I had to tell Marah." He sighed. "She didn't take it super well because she felt like I . . ." He took in a deep breath. "She felt like I wasn't being truthful with her, and . . . yeah. Since we weren't married, she was sort of like, 'Well, I don't have to stay with you.'"

I remembered that he'd transferred seminaries, but he hadn't told me why.

"Oh, so, that's why you transferred?"

"Yeah."

"I had no idea, man. I'm sorry you felt like you couldn't tell anyone, and I'm sorry that it ended that way."

"It's not your fault."

"What did you think when Chris and Megan got pregnant?"

"Oh, dude, that made it all worse, to be honest."

My chest burned for him. "Wait, why?"

"Uh . . ." He let out something between a chuckle and a sob. "Because they made it right by following through with the pregnancy."

"Is that—why did you actually become a pastor?"

"To be completely honest, I thought I'd feel better about my relationship with God."

"Do you?"

"Not in the way you may think. I've realized it is not about me or my mistakes, but about who God is and who Jesus is, and I've realized I still want to be a pastor to undo this stupid lie Christians believe: that despite the cross, they still have to make it right with God, and that there are still sins that God won't redeem or that make you less than."

"Preach, brother."

"I don't know. We'll see."

"Why do you hesitate?"

"Because people are awful. I love the church I'm at—like, I love the pastor—but just because she took me in with open arms does not mean the congregation has, so I'm probably not going to get an offer there, and I don't really want to go back to Ames, which is what my dad wants me to do."

"Have you told your parents?"

"About the abortion?"

"Yeah."

"No."

"Do you think you will?"

"I don't think I have the heart to tell them." He sighed. "I don't know if you know this, but my dad has stage two pancreatic cancer."

"No," I said quietly. "Man, I'm sorry." Keaton's dad was a pastor at our church, and he was a really good role model to me, especially because my dad was barely in my life.

"It is what it is."

"Is he gonna be okay?" I asked him, not sure if it was too intrusive.

"Um . . ." I heard him move over the phone as he sighed. "Honestly? The statistics aren't great."

"Keaton." I said his name, but I didn't know why.

"What?"

"What are the statistics?"

"I don't know for sure, but . . ." He struggled to find words.

I braced myself.

"He has, like, two years," Keaton stated.

What do you say to that? The idea of Pastor Kent not being at church or around anymore? No. Screw death. But that was why we needed the cross.

"I—that's tough."

"Yeah." His voice was tight.

"I'm going to say this, and it may not be the right thing to say, but I think you need to tell your dad about the abortion."

"It'd break his heart, Ten."

"If you had a son and he came to you with that, how would you react?"

"I'd be sad he didn't tell me, or that he thought there was no way out, or that he didn't feel like I was a safe place to catch him after he fell."

"Why didn't you tell your parents?"

He didn't say anything for a moment. "I underestimated them, and now it's too late to open that wound."

"Is the wound healed?"

"Yes, but I think it healed wrong."

"Would telling your parents about what happened lighten the weight?"

He cleared his throat. "Maybe. Or it could just blow up in my face."

"What's the worst that could happen?"

"They disown me. Or they think they were bad parents, and they're not." His voice grew raspy.

"You can still tell them."

"I don't know. I just didn't want to be the pastor's kid who got a girl pregnant, especially given the fact neither she nor I wanted to keep it."

"How long did it take you guys to decide to abort the baby?"

"A few days."

"Did anyone know at the time?"

"Nope."

"Who was the first person you told?" I wondered if he had at least told *someone*. But I was supposed to be the best man in his wedding, and I hadn't even known.

"My mentor."

"The one who reported you," I stated.

"Yeah."

"Wow, so the first time you told someone, you got kicked out of seminary?"

"Yeah."

"Dude, that's awful. I'm sorry. I'm sorry you felt like you couldn't tell anyone, too, and thank you for telling me now."

"Thanks for listening," he told me.

"Yeah, of course. I care a lot about you, and I'm—I really hope you've found friends in L.A. you can trust. I hope you're surrounding yourself with community, but if you ever need to talk, please reach out."

"Thank you, Tennyson." He cleared his throat. "Anyway, what's up with you?"

"Well, I told the guys about quitting."

"And?"

"It was tough, man."

"How'd Austin take it?"

"Well, I told him first—and, man, he's—I'm worried about him."

"Why?"

"He mentioned he didn't know how much longer he could tour. I think being on the road is finally getting to him." Thinking about Austin shot a wave of anxiety through me.

"Makes sense. Single parent on his own."

"It was like me quitting encouraged him to start thinking about it, too."

"Quit?"

"Yeah."

"How does he not get emotional on stage?" Curiosity surrounded his voice.

"I don't know. He's not a very emotional dude, and he's just been kind of detached lately. I think he just doesn't know how to handle everything."

"Fair enough. Have you guys found a replacement yet?"

"No. You interested?" I was kidding around.

"Well, I've actually thought about it."

I felt my eyes widen, even though he couldn't see me. "And?"

"I can't stop thinking about it."

"Well, then maybe that's something to pay attention to."

"I feel like I'm too old these days."

"You're not." I paused. "But maybe you should go be with your family."

"Mhmm, I don't know."

"Come on, man, you should be with your dad."

"I don't want to be a pastor in Ames. I only want to be a pastor if I'm called to a church."

"Do you think you're called to a church in general?"

"Not right now."

"Why?"

"I honestly don't know. I know I won't ever find a perfect church, but I think I need a break for a while. I actually called to ask if you still needed someone to take your spot."

"I think you need to talk to your family first," I said quietly, "and then we can talk."

"Okay."

22

AUSTIN

"Keaton!" I answered, surprised he was calling me. I was laying in my bed, watching Netflix after the girls were finally asleep. "What's going on?" I paused the show.

"Oh, ya know, just doing all the things."

"All the things?"

"Yeah, like finishing up seminary and stuff."

"Oh, yeah." I paused. "What are you doing after seminary?"

"Well, I heard there was a band called GreenButton that needed a drummer."

"Um, yeah! You wanna do it?"

"Yeah."

"I actually forgot you can drum," I confessed.

"Me too. I don't do it very much, but I would hold y'all together."

"I bet you would."

"Is that a job offer?"

"I mean, we'd really be scraping the bottom of the barrel," I said as a joke, "but sure."

"Have you looked at anyone else?"

"Not really. You're the only name that's come up. Tennyson said you mentioned it. But he also mentioned your dad, and I don't want to keep you from being with your family." It had been devastating to hear Pastor Kent was sick.

"Well . . ." He cleared his throat. "He's doing okay right now."

"That's good, but I don't want to keep you stuck on tour if you need to be with your family."

"Says you," he said to me.

"What do you mean?"

"What do you think I mean?" he asked me.

I knew what he was getting at, but I didn't answer. "I don't want you to regret not being around your family if you need to be."

"Austin," he said.

"What?"

"How are *you* away from your family after everything?" Though I don't think he intended it, he sounded judgmental.

"By a bus most of the time," I said dryly.

"Austin," he said again.

"What?"

He didn't say anything.

"So, you wanna go back on the road with us or not?"

"I do, but I don't think it would be long-term."

"Okay, that's fair enough."

"I'll do it until y'all find someone better."

"Why do you wanna do it now then?"

"I just want time away from the church for a while before jumping into long-term ministry."

That seemed weird to me. "Why?"

"I don't know. I just do."

"Are you burned out already?"

"No, not really. This would give me time to figure out the congregation I'm called to."

"Do you not want to work in Ames?" I asked.

"No. And if one more person asks me that, I will move out of the country." He was joking but with genuine frustration in his voice.

"I get it."

"So, my contract at the church ends on December 31."

"Great, we'll be on tour in January. You could move in with Sam." I was kidding.

"Sam Lowe?"

"Yeah."

"Isn't he like twenty?"

"He's twenty-one now."

"How old does he act?"

"Depends on the day."

"I'd consider it."

"Okay, well, I'll tell the band you want to take Tennyson's spot."

"How much longer do you think you'll be touring?" he wondered.

"Like in general?"

"Yeah. Are you wanting to do a long-term thing?"

"Man, I don't know." I really didn't. But the fact he was asking what everyone else was thinking made me shift uncomfortably on the bed as I stared at the paused TV.

*   *   *

Tennyson's last show was a Christmas show. We gave him an MP3 player with a green button as a going-away present. I was sad to see him leave, and we gave speeches about how much we'd miss him and everything, but for me, it was more about wondering if Tennyson leaving to be with his family was what I was supposed to be doing. It was strange that he wouldn't be on the road anymore. I found it kind of difficult to speak about Tennyson. Elena, even. It wasn't like I'd never see them again, but Tennyson had been in the band for a decade through thick and thin, and Elena had toured with us for a bit. Tennyson was one of my best friends. To know this chapter in his life was ending was disheartening.

23

SAM

"**I** know things have been kind of in disarray with GreenButton," Uncle Mike said, walking in and handing me a beer.

"Thank you." I was finally legal. "And yeah," I said quietly.

Ali was sitting on the other end of the couch, drinking a glass of champagne Aunt Lisa had given her. I needed a beer after driving fifteen hours. It was late, but Aunt Lisa had made us cinnamon rolls, and I had eaten a late dinner right outside of Houston. The beer wouldn't hydrate me, though.

"How is the lead singer holding up?" Uncle Mike sat down in the chair.

Maybe it was because I was exhausted from driving all day, or maybe it was because I had fifteen hours to stew in my thoughts, but I knew I was going to choke up as soon as he asked that. Sighing, I said, "He's hanging in there." I kept my voice low.

"How are the rest of you?" Aunt Lisa asked me.

I refused to shed a tear, because then they'd make a big deal out of it, so I took a sip of beer instead. "I think—I mean, it felt like losing a sister—" I put a hand up, remembering who I was talking to. Mike had lost a sister, my mother. "—not that it's the same, but . . ." Looking down in shame, I said, "Sorry if that was insensitive."

"No, not at all." He patted the air with his hand. "She must've meant a lot to you."

Staring up at the ceiling, I focused on my breathing, because he was right. The whole thing sucked. Watching him wipe his eye, my heart fell into my stomach.

Rubbing my nose, I shook my head, not feeling twenty-one. More like twelve. Maybe it was my green silicone dinosaur phone case—or the reality that I was the youngest person in the room by a long shot.

When I looked over at Ali, her beady brown eyes floating in tears, my heart fell again, even though it was normal to see her cry. "Are you okay?" My voice changed into the higher pitch I used with people I didn't know very well and felt obligated to impress. Or the tone I used at the coffee shop I worked at.

Nodding, she gave me a smile, but she still didn't say anything. Her brown eyes were highlighted by red rims. I wanted to hug her, but she probably didn't want to hug me. I wasn't even sure if she knew Cara's name.

When I wasn't in Texas, where I'd grown up, or even in Iowa, where Ali and I had lived, I was able to block out what had happened. Here, at my aunt and uncle's, my past was written all over everything: I couldn't escape. I wasn't supposed to be staying at my aunt and uncle's during the holidays; I was supposed to be at my parents' right now. I let my mind forget it for most of the year, but not here. Maybe Cara's death made it hit harder this year, as my heart was heavy for Austin, and my heart was heavy for the sister I'd known and lost.

My biological sister—who I didn't know—was here, even after what had happened. We were supposed to catch each other when we fell. Far from it. We hugged in greetings and asked how the other was doing, but that was the extent of our relationship. So even though I knew something was off, I didn't want to push.

Taking in a deep breath, not wanting to talk about me anymore, I asked Mike and Lisa, "How have y'all been?"

We engaged in small talk for a little bit, but after a while, Mike called it a night. Ali and I went upstairs as usual, but we didn't talk. I showered, because—well, it was an excuse to be away from Ali as she got ready for bed.

Mike and Lisa's house was huge. It had an upstairs with two mirroring bedrooms, a media area, and a loft. There were two bathrooms on opposite sides, and the bedrooms each had window nooks with built-in benches. There were also built-in desks right next to the sliding door that separated our rooms. After my shower, I sat at the built-in desk because it made me feel like I was in college like I was supposed to be.

As I was messing around on my laptop, I heard quiet sobbing coming through the wall that separated my room from Ali's. No light shone under the crack of the door, so I figured she was trying to sleep. If the tables were turned, she wouldn't check in on me. In fact, the tables had been turned before. My first Christmas after I'd been in the band, I'd been really excited to see Ali, and maybe it had been ignorant of me to think things would be different.

Though I couldn't even remember what was said now, she called me out for something that had made me feel really small, so I had excused myself upstairs. When no one came to check on me, I realized I wasn't sure if my family even cared about me.

*   *   *

The next day was Christmas Eve, so Mike and Lisa's kids, Amber and Lauren, were over. Amber was married to Dean. Amber was Ali's age, and Lauren was about three years older than me.

Amber, Dean, Lauren, Ali, and I played Ticket to Ride. I noticed Ali would make funny comments to the other three, or laugh at what they'd say, but when I said something, she just—she would go silent or blank.

Even though my cousins lived in the area, they were staying the night. They all started getting ready for bed on the main level. Ali headed upstairs, and I followed. I turned the hallway lights on in the loft area.

"Hey," I said quietly, "are you okay?"

"Yeah, I'm fine," she told me bitterly.

"Then why do you give me that tone every time you talk to me?"

"I don't give you a tone." She started toward her room.

"Ali—wait." I caught the door she tried shutting in my face, surprised by the sternness in my voice.

She stared blankly at me as I plucked up the courage to start this uncomfortable conversation. "Are you mad at me?"

Then her look turned into a glare. "Am I mad at you?" She rolled her eyes. "You go around crying about how you lost a sister when you don't even talk to me. You didn't even tell me your band almost broke up because Austin's wife died—you have a sister right here, Sam." Her eyes filled with tears. "I had to find out through social media."

"I didn't want to bother you," I told her.

"But—I shouldn't have found out one of your best friends died through social media."

Staring at the tan carpet, I admitted, "It was super hard to talk about."

"You still should've told me."

"Maybe I would've called you if you had a better track record of being supportive when people die." It was one thing to say things you don't mean when you're upset, but I actually meant every word.

"Like you even gave me a chance," she snapped.

"You blew your chance when you told me Mom and Dad would still be here if I would've just cleaned my room." My words poured out of my mouth through a rising voice.

The silence that followed was the same silence that followed the car accident as I had watched my father die, not even given a chance to say I was sorry. I could still see the red and blue flashing lights of the ambulances and fire trucks as I rode with Mom to the hospital because maybe she still had a chance. She had died on the way. I'd walked away with a broken arm because I'd braced my left arm on the back of Dad's seat. It got bent in a way it wasn't meant to bend. I still had the scar from the surgery on my forearm.

The green sleeve of my sweater had been rolled up while we'd been playing the game, and the raised pink line on my forearm had been visible. It was a reminder this all had really happened.

"I don't remember saying that," she told me quietly. "And I don't know what would make me say that. And I'm sorry—I'm sorry if I did." She stared blankly at me for a moment, but then she asked, "You really think I blame you, Sam?" Her voice was quiet.

"I don't know, Ali, you never talk to me." I forced amusement.

"And I could say the same about you, Sam."

"Why would I want to talk to you?" I mumbled.

"What have I done to you, Sam?" she snapped.

"Nothing. That's the problem," I tossed back.

"You pushed me away. You don't even tell me when the band is in Iowa half the time. I tried to be there for you, but you never wanted to talk. I took care of you. I made sure you were fed and clothed. I went to your games and performances—"

"—yeah, like three times," I scoffed.

"Look, I showed up for you. I did everything I could, given what resources I had, and if it wasn't enough, I'm sorry, because I did the best I could." Her voice broke and her tears did, too. After she slammed the door in my face, I looked over the dark living room from the loft, resting my elbows on the black railing, fighting back the silent tears, thinking to myself how beautiful the layout of this house was as I focused on my breathing. I wouldn't cry over this when I seldom wept for my parents.

When I heard her come out of her room, I didn't even flinch.

"Okay, I'm sorry," she said.

Not knowing how to fix it—we'd both said some pretty destructive things—I took in a deep breath. "I'm sorry, too," I whispered, not trusting my voice but looking her in the eyes.

She stood next to me, leaning on the railing. The big windows revealed our reflections. She was close to me.

"Do you blame yourself?" she asked as if she had to.

Having to ask myself honestly, I thought about it for the millionth time but for the first time in a while. Would Dad have waited to make that left-hand turn if he hadn't been lecturing me about the chores I'd refused to do? Probably, but that didn't make it my fault, and I knew that. It was just an unfortunate thing. The truck that had hit us was a lot bigger than our car, and it had been speeding. I had an image of Dad with his brownish-gray hair putting a hand on my shoulder and saying, *I would never want you to blame yourself.* I heard his voice in my head, not knowing if that's what his voice had actually sounded like. I still trusted it as I shook my head. "I don't," I told Ali, holding back tears, straightening up, gripping the railing.

"I don't blame you either." She put a hand on my back. "And I'm sorry you thought I did, because I never have."

Nodding, simply to acknowledge her, I thought about where we were and how we'd gotten here.

"And honestly," she added, "it breaks my heart to know you thought I did."

"It breaks my heart that you felt like I pushed you away."

We looked into each other's misty brown eyes. Her dirty blonde hair and mine, the same color brown with strawberry-blond highlights, blended together as we embraced each other. Letting her pull away first, after an extended moment, I took in her tearstained face. I couldn't bring myself to let go in front of her.

"I want my brother back," she said aloud.

Nodding, I bit my lip, and I pulled her into another embrace, heartbroken about the time lost but leery about whether anything would be changed tomorrow.

"I want to know what's going on in your life and how you really are," she told me genuinely, which meant a lot—more than words could express. I could've bawled.

Being raw with her felt so foreign. Was it too little too late?

When we said goodnight for the second time, I went back to the room, sunk onto my bed, and texted Mo.

Hey Ali and I just got into a really rough talk and I don't really wanna talk tonight. Sorry.

Thats fine. Are you ok?

Yeah Ill be ok

Are you ok now?

Eh I just dont wanna talk bout it

Ok well I'm here for you when you need to talk.

Thanks

I paced the room slowly, debating whether I had it in me to let go. I was afraid if I did let go, the tears might never stop. I didn't want Ali to hear me. So, I just paced in the heaviness.

24

AUSTIN

"NANA! NANA!" Bella screamed as we were playing UNO. I handed my cards to Leo, my brother. "Play for me."

"He has all green cards," Leo announced, lying because I only had one green card. The rest were blue. The cards hadn't been shuffled well.

"Nana!" Bella cried out again.

"I'm coming, baby girl," I told her, and I started up the steps, surrounded by sage-green walls inside and out. The tan carpet squished underneath my socks.

I opened the door, and when I walked in, Kaleigha said, "Daddy, I want Nana."

Bella was still crying, so I picked her up. "Nana, Nana, Nana."

"Why do you want Nana?" I whispered to Kaleigha. I sat on the edge of the twin bed in Leo's old room, wiping Bella's cheeks with my thumbs before she rested her face against my shoulder.

"Toys."

"At Nana's?" I spoke above a whisper.

"Yeah." Kaleigha rested her head on my knee.

"Nana," Bella said.

"I'm Dadda, ya silly goose," I told Bella. "Kaleigha, you got new toys today!" I told her. "And you know Santa's coming tonight, so you gotta sleep, because there will be presents when you wake up!"

"How does Santa get through the chimney if he eats lotsa cookies?" Kaleigha asked.

"I don't know, to be honest, kiddo. I've seen him come through the fireplace, but I don't remember how he did it."

"I wanna see him."

"Yeah, but if he knows you're up, waiting for him, he'll have to wait to come to Iowa, so you need to go to sleep, okay?"

"Fine."

When I tried putting Bella back down in the crib, she screamed, "No!"

"Hey," I whispered. "Let's go to sleep." I left her in the crib, offering her my hand to cling onto. "I love you." When I took away my hand to leave the room, Bella cried out.

"I'm scared, Daddy," Kaleigha then told me.

"Why?"

"I don't like this house."

"Why not?"

"Dark," Kaleigha told me.

"Would it help if I left the hallway light on?"

I started out again as she said, "Yeah."

Bella cried as I went into the hallway to flip the light on. When I came back, I sat on the floor, next to Bella's crib. If this was our house, then I wouldn't stay with her, but this place was strange to her. "I'll stay here for a while until Bella calms down, but no talking," I whispered. "I love you, Kaleigha."

Bella calmed down pretty quickly, but I stayed for about ten minutes, hoping she'd fall asleep. Quietly, I crept up and left, leaving the door open a crack.

"Hey, y'all," I said when I got down, "the door to the girls' room is open to let in the hallway light, so if we could keep it quiet, that'd be great." I sat next to Leo.

"You lost," Leo told me.

"We started a new game because we don't like you," Luke informed me.

"Wow. Who won?"

Mom glared at me, pressing her lips together.

"What?" I asked her.

"What do you think, Austin?"

"I don't know—why are you giving me that look?"

She pressed her glasses up the bridge of her nose. "Your kids want your mother-in-law instead of you," she told me.

"Mom," Luke said quietly.

"That's not true," I said over Luke.

"It is true." She didn't skip a beat. "We heard both of them call for her."

"Kaleigha misses the toys at Donna's house."

"What about Bella?"

"She—I don't know, but she's fine."

"She's fine if she's calling for 'Nana' instead of 'Dadda'?" She was trying not to yell.

"Mom," Luke warned again.

"What's your point?" I asked.

"Your kids don't even want you. That's my point."

"Brenda." Dad put a hand on her shoulder. "That's kind of unfair."

"Okay." I looked at her. "When I am home, it's during the day, and I get to be with them for extended periods of time."

"They shouldn't want their grandparents more than you."

"You're just jealous they're able to spend more time with them."

"No, I'm embarrassed my son is rarely home with his kids and that they want their Nana more than him. That's embarrassing."

"Brenda, stop," Dad said calmly.

"It's not like I'm gone because I'm dealing drugs. I'm gone because I'm spreading the news about Jesus."

"That's great. Become a worship pastor. You can be home at night and tell people about Jesus."

"It's not that simple."

"Why not?" Leo asked me matter-of-factly.

"Because the label would cancel our record deal."

"And what would happen if they did?" Mom asked.

"Then we would struggle to produce music. To market it."

"So, producing music and touring is more important to you than being home with your kids," Mom stated.

"That's not what I said, Mom." I put a hand up.

"Actions speak louder than words, kid. It doesn't matter your intention. Your kids lost their mom, and they need you home."

"Even when Cara was alive, you hated that I toured," I snapped a little louder than intended.

"And lo and behold, you weren't there when she needed you the most."

That one cut.

"Okay, you know what?" I slammed the table before getting up. "Nothing I do will ever be enough for you." I turned away, my lip trembling. I fought the tears, because I'd never seen my older brothers or father cry, so they wouldn't see it from me either.

I headed upstairs because I just wanted to be alone. Spike followed me into my old room, and I shut the door behind us, stumbling over to the bed, fighting back the tears just in case someone came up. Spike curled up on the bed, and I held onto him, staring up at the ceiling of my bedroom. I would not cry. Not here. I prayed, *God, help me. I don't know what to do. I'm sorry. Help me. Help me. Help me. I suck. It's my fault.*

Someone knocked on my door. I ignored them. "Dude, I'm coming in." Luke walked in. "Hey," he said quietly, shutting the door behind him.

I avoided his eyes.

"You wanna go see the new restaurant?" Luke and I had already discussed visiting his new restaurant while I was in town.

"Right now?" My voice was hoarse.

"Yeah. The night is young."

"I'll get yelled at for not being around for my kids," I mumbled. My voice tightened as I started tearing up again.

"Ya know what? The hardest thing Mom's ever experienced is raising kids who didn't graduate from college, so no wonder she doesn't get it." Only Leo had graduated college—then law school. He'd met his wife there, too. Luke put a light hand on my back. "Are you okay?" Luke was a big, burly dude with a thick beard, sporting tattoos up and down his arms. His deep voice boomed with genuine concern.

I shrugged.

He wrapped an arm around me.

I swallowed back tears. "We should go see your restaurant," I said to him.

"Okay."

He got up, and I followed him, wiping my eyes behind him. When we got downstairs, Luke announced, "Hey, I'm gonna show Austin the restaurant."

I grabbed my GreenButton navy jacket from the closet, flaunting our logo in the top corner. For Iowa, it wasn't super cold, so I figured I'd be fine with just a jacket. I double checked my pockets for my phone.

Slipping on my shoes, I didn't even look in Mom or Dad's direction. I followed Luke outside. The cold air penetrated my light jacket, but I wasn't about to go back into that house. I thought about talking about everything, but I couldn't bring myself to admit how depressed I was. In fact, I hardly said anything to Luke as he showed me his newest achievement.

* * *

"I'm gonna grab the presents," Liz, Leo's wife, said after a long game of Pitch that we all stayed up for, including Mom.

"Oh, shoot," I said, "I need to do that, too."

"Where'd you hide yours?" Liz asked me.

"Underneath the passenger's seat of my car." I kept my voice quiet just in case young ears were listening.

"Classic."

"I'm gonna go get them," I said, getting up, grabbing the keys from the key rack. It was the same key rack I'd used in high school, but it wasn't mine anymore. When I had lived with my parents, it was as if everything that was theirs was mine, but now that I had my own house and life, I was a guest in their house. I popped through their garage, past Mom and Dad's vehicles, and made my way to the street where my car was.

I checked underneath the front passenger seat—nothing was there. My heart dropped into my stomach. It was eleven o'clock on Christmas Eve. What was I going to do? The presents I'd bought my little girls were not there. I lost them, like the bad dad I was. Kaleigha would be so upset if Liam had presents and she didn't. I grabbed my phone to illuminate the space below the seat. They just weren't there.

I remembered putting them there. Had they been stolen? I shouldn't have left them in the car, but I did.

I checked the backseat. I checked the glove compartment that was too small anyway. I checked underneath the driver's seat. I checked the trunk. I even checked where the spare tire lived. Nothing. Where could they have gone? Those presents were the one thing I was supposed to do right this Christmas.

Breathe. Breathe. Breathe. *It's not the end of the world. You're fine. You're fine. You're fine.*

I gripped the top of my hatchback, fighting back tears as the cold stung my eyes.

If Cara were here, this would not be happening. She'd ensure they'd have their presents in the right place.

Catching tears with my palms, I considered going on a walk. It was cold. But I couldn't go back into that house, because I was going to cry if they asked why I'd come back empty handed.

So I got in the car and started driving. I didn't have my wallet, but I had my phone.

I didn't want to cry on Christmas Eve. It was a holiday, a day that was supposed to be good. Jesus was born, meaning I would be able to see Cara again, assuming all of this was real. Cara had loved Christmas—I didn't want to think about her because I missed her too much. What Mom had said was a little true. It had been made pretty clear tonight that my kids wanted Donna. If I walked back into that house empty handed, my mom would think even worse of me.

As I drove around Ames, I took in the rare silence and lack of traffic. This had been my home before Cara, my home before my innocence had been stripped from me in college. Things had been simpler here. Not anymore. I wasn't enough for my mom. Or my kids. What the hell was I supposed to do with that?

Everything was wrong. I thought about what would happen if I were to jump off a bridge. My kids might be better off with people who wanted to be home with them.

That wasn't true though. And I knew that.

But I had nothing left. Nothing left to give.

I started to cry.

And I couldn't bring myself to listen to my uneven breathing, so I turned on the local radio, thankful for familiar songs despite their constant reminders of Santa Claus.

I'd heard a hundred stories of people hitting rock bottom, meaning they'd lived to tell about it. I wasn't thinking clearly, so I drove home to my parents' house; I didn't want to be alone. Wiping my eyes before getting out, I planned out what to say if I'd get asked questions: the truth.

They needed to know.

When I walked in, most of my family was standing in the doorway.

"Where were you?" Mom demanded.

"I went on a drive."

"Why didn't you tell us?" Leo sounded concerned.

"Um . . ." I folded my arms, looking down at the tile. "Don't hate me, but I couldn't find the presents from Santa." My voice was quiet.

"Austin," Mom said, "we were worried about you."

Was I not allowed to leave?

Leo wrapped an arm around me. "Why didn't you answer our calls?"

"You called?" I hadn't felt my phone vibrate.

"Yeah," Leo said. "Luke is driving around looking for you."

"Why?" Now, I felt a little guilty.

"Because you left without saying goodbye at 11:00 on Christmas Eve," Leo said.

"I'm sorry."

"I'm gonna call Luke." Dad paused. "I'm glad you're okay." He squeezed my shoulder.

"And I'm sorry about what I said earlier," Mom told me.

"You still mean it," I mumbled.

"I still think you should be home, but I recognize you just don't want to lose your wife and job with the same stone."

I didn't want to talk about any of it anymore, no matter how much sense she made. A tear splattered onto the oak hardwood floor that I stared down at.

Leo squeezed my shoulders.

"I'm gonna head to bed," I announced.

Leo stepped back to let Mom embrace me. I didn't hug her back.

"I love you so much," she whispered. "I'm sorry you're going through this." I lost my kids' presents, and she wasn't yelling at me. That shouldn't have been as much of a surprise or relief as it was. Even though I wasn't looking at her, I could hear she was close to tears.

I twisted away from Mom.

"Love you, man." Leo pulled me into a hug.

"I'm glad you're safe." Liz embraced me.

Tears rolled as I blinked, so I pulled away from her.

Dad hung up with Luke, and then he wrapped his arms around me before I had a chance to dab my face.

"I'm glad you're okay," Dad told me. "We love you."

I was not okay, but I was alive. Maybe that was enough right now.

When I got into my room, I shut the door behind me and started crying again. I had heard the fear in their voices, and I knew they cared. I thought about what would've happened if I'd jumped off a bridge, how devastated everyone would have been. I knew the pain of losing someone prematurely, and I didn't want to put that on anyone else.

A few minutes later, I heard a knock on my door, so I quickly tried to mop my flooded cheeks with the cuffs of my jacket. Dad walked in without warning as I sat up on my bed. He sat on the edge, wrapping his hand around my bicep even though he wasn't an extremely touchy person. "So, why did you drive away?" he asked matter-of-factly.

"I didn't want to have to tell Mom I couldn't find the presents," I whispered.

"Where did you go?"

"I just drove around," I told him.

"Were you going anywhere?"

"No. Nothing is open."

"It seemed kind of out of character for you to leave without telling us where you were going," he told me.

"Yeah, I'm sorry. I just—I didn't . . ." I wouldn't have hurt myself. But I understood why they'd been concerned. To ease his fears, I told him the truth: "I didn't want to be told I was a horrible parent again." My voice tightened into a whisper.

"You're not."

"Some would disagree," I mumbled.

"I don't think you are."

"Mom does." A tear that I forgot to fight slipped. Swiping it away quickly, I gripped my face, staring at the closed blind so he couldn't see my face.

Dad squeezed my neck. "Hey. No, she doesn't. She just thinks you need to be home with your kids. That does not equate to you being a horrible parent."

When I didn't respond, he pulled me close. I covered my damp face with both of my hands, hearing something between a snuffle and sob come out of me. I realized if I let him hold me, I would completely lose it. I pulled away, lifting my face, staring straight ahead at the closed door that led into the walk-in closet. "I'm sorry."

"No, I'm sorry that you've had a rough night—rough year."

"It's not your fault," I said quietly. But maybe it was my fault. I hadn't been there when Cara had needed me most.

We sat in the silence as I willed myself to pull it together.

"What can I do?" he finally asked me.

"Just tell me if Mom's right." I sniffed, wiping the moisture from my hands onto my jeans.

"About what?"

"Should I still tour?"

"That's not her call to make. Or mine. I do think you put your identity into the band, and now you're holding on so tight because you don't want to lose something else." He moved his hand to my shoulder to pat it. "Which is kind of disheartening, because I know better than anyone you're good at a lot of things."

"Like what?" Bitterness surrounded my voice.

"Well, already, you *are* a good dad."

"They want their nana more than me."

"I don't think that's true. I've seen the way you interact with Kaleigha and Bella. They adore you and love hanging around you. You know that, Austin. And they should like their nana, too. That's normal." Then he whispered, "I think your mom's just jealous of Donna."

I took in a slow, deep breath. That was the issue: my baby girls missed and wanted me, and I still chose to tour. And I didn't want to even think about the way Mom had chastised me for not being home when Cara had taken her last breath, so I asked Dad, "So, what do I do about the Christmas presents?"

He squinted his gray eyebrows and then stood up. "Wait." He walked over to the walk-in closet and said, "You mean the ones you told me to sneak in?"

I followed him in, and sure enough, on the top shelf, there were a dozen presents wrapped up in pink and aqua-green wrapping paper.

Oh, yeah.

"Oh. I'm dumb."

"If touring doesn't work out, maybe you should go to college," he teased, caressing my back.

I gave him an amused smile.

"I'll help you bring them down."

Mom and Luke were standing in the kitchen when Dad and I came down. Their silence made me wonder if they'd been talking about me.

"Found 'em." My voice cracked.

"Yay!" Mom said.

"Hey, you're alive," Luke told me. "You gave me a heart attack."

"Yeah, sorry," I told him.

"I thought you ran away." He said it in a joking manner, but there's always some truth in sarcasm.

"I wouldn't do that."

He studied my face but nodded hesitantly.

"Where were the presents?" Mom asked.

Dad and I exchanged glances, and we both burst into laughter.

25

AUSTIN

The tiny chocolate chips mixed with the little ice chunks in my drink reminded me of how the roads in Iowa were when the snow melted, how the salt and the mud would mix with the white snow, making a cookies and cream concoction. That was the only way I could consume coffee—by drowning it in milk. Even in Michigan, even in the bitter cold, I also hated hot drinks because I was never patient enough to avoid burning my tongue.

"Did you actually get kicked out of seminary?" I asked Keaton, forcing nonchalance just in case he wasn't kidding.

"Doesn't surprise me," Riley told him. "Pastor's kid has to go through some sort of crisis."

Keaton didn't smile. "Yeah." Keaton sat next to Sam, who peered at him.

"What did you do?" Riley didn't believe him.

Keaton looked at him. "I got a girl pregnant when I was studying at Iowa, and then I paid for the abortion. After several years of not dealing with it, I figured I should tell my mentor and practice what I was beginning to preach—you know, be vulnerable about the things that have shaped you. So I did, and then he told the dean of students, and they asked me to leave, so then I transferred to another seminary." I had known Keaton a long time, and he had a way of watering down serious situations.

Nobody knew what to say to that.

"They kicked you out for something that happened while you were in college?" Chris was pissed.

"Yeah."

"Have you met Chris and Megan?" Riley mumbled.

Chris ignored Riley's comment.

We had been in a band together for years—how did I not know? He had admitted he'd given up the party scene, but that was it. I didn't complain because he'd transferred to UNI his junior year, my freshman year, so having him around meant we could do band-related things up at school.

"At least you guys did the right thing," Keaton said quietly to Chris. "I didn't."

"By keeping the babies?" Chris asked quietly.

"Yeah." Keaton didn't meet any of our eyes as he rolled up the wrapper from my straw.

"That—that must've been a big burden to carry," Chris told him. "And I'm sorry that when you were ready to tell someone, they betrayed your trust."

"It's whatever. He was just trying to do the right thing."

"I don't hold any judgment toward you or the girl for making that choice," Chris said to him.

"Yeah, things happen, man," Riley said.

"Thank you for being open with us," Chris said to him.

Keaton took a sip of his black coffee. Whenever his cheeks reddened, whether from running, warmth, or embarrassment, they looked like stoplights on his smooth face.

"I wish everyone was as gracious as you guys."

"Who all knows?"

"The pastor I interned for, and she was really graceful about it." Then he paused. "And Marah."

"What did Marah say?" Chris asked.

"She called off the engagement," Keaton leaned back in his chair uncomfortably. "But it's fine; I'm over it." He cleared his throat.

"So, your family doesn't know," Chris stated.

"They don't." He pulled his lips into his mouth.

"Will you . . . ?" Chris pushed.

"I don't know." Keaton cleared his throat again. His hazel eyes grew misty all of a sudden.

"It might bring healing that you need," Sam stated.

Keaton gave him a smile. "I don't know if they need to know. I don't think my dad would benefit from that kind of news."

"You can sit in your own convictions, but I think your parents would want to know," Chris said.

"Why?" he asked

"Because it still bothers you," Chris told him. "And your dad knows what grace is, and he'd want to show you that too."

"Yeah, but my mom would be heartbroken that she didn't meet her grandchild." His voice broke.

"Either way," Riley said, "it wasn't your choice to make."

"It wasn't, but I paid for the procedure."

"Okay," I said, "look, women get abortions. Whether you paid for it or not, whether it's right or wrong, it happened, and there's nothing you can do about it now, but being open about it with your family might help you heal. But thank you for being open with us." I almost added, "I still look at you the same way." But I didn't. This person I thought I'd known really well was carrying this burden, and it reminded me that even pastors carry stuff. I wasn't the only one. I wasn't sure if it made my situation better or not because my throat was suddenly very tight.

He nodded, stroking his blond eyebrows. "Thank you."

That tightness followed me throughout the rest of the day.

* * *

We were on tour with Resin Ring to make up shows we hadn't been able to complete the year before. They were an older band, but we were a little more known. Both Hannah and Valerie were married with young kids, so they understood we needed to be strategic with scheduling.

We decided to have them join the Q&A with us this tour because we figured that would redirect attention away from us. People could be really intrusive, so we would encourage questions both Resin Ring and GreenButton could answer.

But one guy with jet-black hair, probably around Sam's age, said, "I know this isn't a question, but I just want to say that 'Bigger' probably saved my life, because it made me realize God really is bigger than grief and doubts and questions, and I just want to thank you for writing that song. I know you've been through a lot in the past year, and it probably wasn't easy. I just want you to know something good came out of that." I didn't know what the guy's voice usually sounded like, but I could tell by its tremor that the song was emotional for him to talk about.

"Thank you. That means a lot."

A year ago, if someone had told me a song had saved their life, I'd have gotten emotional. To know that something you created had an impact on someone was definitely humbling.

But tonight, it didn't seem to matter that much. Nothing seemed to matter.

26

CHRIS

I'm alone tonight
With no hope in sight,
No will to fight anymore.
"I hear all these stories
About people having a moment
When they come to You
I want one too
But it seems like I can't trust You
Because I'm struggling
And juggling
All these things.
"Oh, Jesus, let me trust You
I want to so badly
I would gladly take it
Sadly I can't feel it.
"Oh, Lord, I can't handle this anymore
People tore me up to shreds

And I can't wrap my head around the fact
That You allow them to hurt Your beloved
Can't you at least mend my heart?"

Austin choked on the words of the bridge. "*Oh, Lord, let me trust You,*" he tried to sing. "*I want to—*" He sounded out of breath, so he pointed the mic at the audience, but the audience didn't know the words, which made it even worse. They started cheering instead. I kept playing as I walked over to him. "*I would gladly take it. Sadly, I can't feel it.*" He couldn't hit the high notes, but he kept playing his guitar. His lip trembled. Not even surprised this was happening—it was bound to happen at some point—I put a hand on his shoulder, which meant I was no longer playing, and I thought about singing, but I lost track of where we were in the song. He turned away from the audience.

No. I wrapped an arm around him, surprised he wasn't sweaty. He was shaking. Austin covered his face, and the crowd started cheering louder. People were like, "We love you, Austin!" Sam took over the song, but it took a moment for Sam's mic to be turned up.

"Breathe. Breathe," I said to him as he hyperventilated.

I could only hold him.

I don't know how he did it, but he finished the song. It didn't sound very good, but he did it. Then he did two more songs, not mentioning what had just happened. When we finished our last song, Austin scurried off the stage as fast as he could. He ripped off his guitar, putting it back in the case, just backstage.

"Are you okay?" I asked him.

He responded, but I couldn't hear what he said over the applause. I quickly put my guitar back in its case, too. Putting a very light hand on Austin's shoulder as he headed out backstage, I asked him, "Hey. Are you okay?"

He just shook his head. Usually, we'd hang out wherever our stuff was or watch the show, but he didn't seem to be moving in that direction. He walked toward the stairs in the direction the bus was parked, next to the lower level.

"Where are you going?"

He stuffed his hands in the pockets of his jeans, staring straight ahead as we walked.

"Can you talk to me?" I pleaded.

"I don't know," he snapped.

"What's wrong?" I asked him quietly.

"I don't know what happened." His voice broke as he folded his arms.

"What do you mean?"

"I couldn't breathe out there, Chris."

I forced myself to look into his misty blue eyes.

"I didn't even know if I was going to get through the set. I don't know what's wrong." He made an effort to hold back his tears as he held his chin with his shaking hand.

"You did get through it." My voice was quiet.

"Barely," he mumbled.

"But you did."

He leaned against the wall.

"What are you thinking about right now?"

He kept his gaze on the floor. "That was so embarrassing."

"What was?"

"Not being able to get through a set."

"You were resilient, though." He really was.

"It wasn't good."

"It also wasn't bad." If you didn't know his normal singing voice, it really was fine.

"It was bad, man." He cleared his throat, sighing.

"What made you upset?"

"I don't know."

"Really? You just break down on stage for no reason?"

He took in a deep breath, shrugging, looking away as he continued to fight it.

"You're shaking, buddy." I squeezed his shoulder and wrapped a hand around his arm. The dude had some muscle. "Talk to me," I whispered.

"I don't know if I believe it anymore, Chris," he whispered.

"Believe what?"

"In God."

"That's a lot to wrestle with."

"What if He's not real?"

"I don't know, what if He's not?"

"Then I won't see Cara again, and it's all meaningless."

"Why do you think God isn't real?"

"Because I've run across people who challenge whether the Bible is really the Word of God, and maybe they're right. And even if He is real, I don't see the point of anything. If our purpose is to glorify God, then isn't that pretty selfish of Him, considering how much brokenness and pain there is in this world?"

"That's a valid question. Do you blame God for Cara's passing?"

"I don't know if 'blame' is the right word."

"What is?"

He cleared his throat. "It's hard because she died serving Him, and He didn't spare her life, which for her, she sort of, in a way, got the better end of the stick. But everyone misses her. I don't think she would've wanted us to feel the pain of missing her, and I don't think she'd want her kids to grow up without a mother." His voice broke, but he kept talking. "So, I guess I don't understand why . . ." He blinked back the moisture in his eyes.

"Why what?"

"He didn't save her, because He could have." His broken voice was small and worn out, but faith remained.

"I don't know why God didn't save Cara either," I told him honestly, holding back my own tears. "You wanna have this conversation on the bus?"

He nodded, sniffling a bit. "Yeah." We started toward the stairs.

"Do you believe in God right now?" I asked after I found my voice again.

"I don't know."

My heart did break a little bit more when he said that. "Okay, that's fine."

"It's actually not, because it's my job."

"It's fine to doubt though. If you don't doubt, then there's no room for faith."

"Why would God make faith the only way to get into Heaven when it's something you can't see?"

"Maybe as a humble reminder that we're not God and He is bigger than our understanding. God is bigger than our questions and doubts."

"It doesn't matter if it's not real."

"What doesn't matter?"

"Anything."

"What do you mean by that?" I asked him quietly.

"If God isn't real, then it's all for nothing."

"What is all for nothing?"

"Everything. Life. It literally doesn't matter."

"Austin, what are you saying?"

"I don't know. That this might all be meaningless." He opened the door and held it for me as I walked through.

"So, what do you do with that?" I asked him.

"I don't even know," he groaned as he led me into the bus after he'd unlocked it with the keypad. Only the sink light was on in the living area. Jimmy, the bus driver, was probably sleeping.

"I mean, are you—are you okay?" I slid into the booth, and he slid in across from me.

"I don't know."

"You sound depressed."

Swallowing hard, his eyes welled up again. "I probably am."

"Are you suicidal?"

Leaning back in the booth, he looked at me. "No. I couldn't do that to you guys or my parents. I would never want you guys to go through what I'm going through right now." His voice shook. "I've seen Donna and Charlie lose a child, and it's devastating. Not to mention, I have kids."

"You know, Riley and I've lost people to suicide," I told him. "And you're right—it's devastating, and I don't think I could handle losing you." I saw what Cara's passing had done to Megan, and though she was resilient, I didn't want to imagine losing Austin.

"Thank you." His voice sounded hoarse.

"I mean that."

Austin nodded, still tearing up. "I know."

"Dude, you're really shaking," I acknowledged again. "Are you scared?"

He shrugged, tapping his mouth with his fist. "I don't even know anymore."

"Okay, how do you feel?"

"Hungry."

"That's an easy fix."

He looked down. "It's hard to eat sometimes."

"What do you mean?"

"Like, my throat gets really tight when I try."

"Didn't you eat dinner?"

"I gagged on a few bites." We'd had sandwiches for dinner.

"Gagged?"

"Yeah, I had to force myself to swallow bites with water."

"Did you eat lunch?"

"I ate maybe half a piece of pizza, and then couldn't do it anymore."

"When was the last time you ate a full meal?"

He thought about it. "Yesterday at lunch; I ate my sandwich at the cafe."

How did I not notice he was barely eating? "What do you feel like when you can't eat?"

"Like my throat is tight."

"Do you have a lump in your throat?"

He played with his fingers, but nodded. "Yeah."

"Do you need to cry?"

"Do I need to cry?" He ran a hand down his face.

"Yeah, do you need to cry?" I asked in a matter-of-fact tone.

"I mean, maybe."

"I see the tears in your eyes." Being this blunt felt intrusive, especially when he avoided eye contact. "Can I ask you a weird question?"

"What?"

"When was the last time you actually cried?"

"Define cry." He licked his lips.

"Like, let go—like, didn't fight it, and just . . . cried?"

He didn't respond. He just sat there.

"Austin."

"Christmas Eve," he finally admitted.

"What happened?"

"Um . . ." He clasped his hands, flashing a smile, rolling his eyes. "I thought I lost the Christmas presents from Santa."

"But you didn't?"

"Nope."

"Did anything else happen?"

"Well . . ." He sighed. "There was a lot happening that night."

"Like what?"

"I don't want to get into it. It wasn't that big of a deal."

In a way, I felt rejected when he pushed back, but I couldn't blame him. "It must've been a big enough deal to make you cry."

"Maybe that's why I don't want to talk about it." He sounded annoyed.

"Can I be honest with you?"

"Sure." He sounded bored.

"I'm worried about you."

"You probably should be," he told me. At least he was honest, too.

"Well, that doesn't make me feel better." That time, I hadn't intended to be as direct.

"Yeah, I know. I'm sorry." He put his hands up. "Seriously, I'm sorry to put this on you."

"No, thank you for telling me. I don't want you to hear that as a negative thing. I just—I want you to talk to someone, though."

Nodding, he mumbled, "That sounds expensive."

"It might be, but look into what our insurance allows, because you've been through a lot, and . . ." It felt like I was talking to him as he was drowning. "You're just not yourself."

"I know, but I don't know if therapy would fix anything," he told me.

"What will fix it?"

He blinked back tears still. "Maybe time?" Austin asked the ceiling. "Maybe nothing."

"Do you think it will get better?"

The distance in his watery blue eyes told me everything I needed to know. "I don't know, and that's the scary part."

"Okay." I took in a deep breath. "I think you need help."

"I know," he finally said.

"On Monday morning, you need to schedule an appointment with a counselor."

"Okay."

"Before you go back to your house, I want to see you call them, and I will drive you, and Megan and I could watch your kids if needed."

He nodded. "Thanks, Chris."

Despite the conversation we had that night, we finished the show with Resin Ring and tabled like normal. No one could tell how rough of a night he was having, but the kid who told us that "Bigger" saved his life grabbed a photo with us.

"Stories like yours remind me why we keep doing this," Austin told him.

*　　*　　*

On Monday, he set up an appointment with a counselor for later that day. I called him that night to check in.

"How'd the first counseling session go?"

"Okay. We think I had a panic attack on stage the other night."

"Oh, that makes sense."

"Yeah, and the counselor thinks my eating problems are related to anxiety."

"I could definitely see that."

"Yeah."

"What else did you talk about?"

"I told him I wanted to be okay and not be anxious or depressed anymore, and he told me if I wasn't anxious or depressed after losing Cara, then that would be more of a concern."

"True. When do you go back?"

"Next Tuesday."

"Good. I'm here for you, too."

"I know. Thank you for making me do this."

27

AUSTIN

The band and I were sitting in a diner that probably hadn't been updated since the 1970s, waiting for food in a little old town in Pennsylvania. When a Nashville number called me, I considered that it could be spam, but I answered anyway. "This is Austin."

"Hi, Austin, this is Barb—one of the teachers at Kaleigha's school." *Uh oh.* I got up and started walking out of the diner. "Kaleigha was pulling down a blind—" The worst went through my head. She probably strangled herself. "—and then the blind fell on her, cutting her forehead—"

"—I want Daddy!" I heard Kaleigha cry. She was alive. "I want Daddy!"

"—It's bleeding. The other teacher has pressure on it, but can you come take her to the ER?"

"Wait, is she okay?"

"She'll be fine. There's just a lot of blood."

Bleeding? Would it be possible for her to bleed out? I knew very little about medical-related things.

"Listen, I'm actually out of state right now, but you can call her grandparents. You should have their contact information, but I can give it to you."

Then she recited Donna's number.

"Yup. If she doesn't pick up, do you have Charlie Minty's number?"

She recited that, too.

"Okay, if they don't pick up, call me back."

"Will do."

"Thanks. Keep me updated."

"Okay."

When I got off the phone, I texted both Donna and Charlie to fill them in. I provided Barb's phone number and asked them to keep me updated.

When I walked back in, Chris asked, "Everything okay?"

"Um, no." I flashed a shy smile, swallowing. "Not really."

"What happened?" Sam asked.

"Kaleigha pulled on a blind at preschool and hit herself in the head. Her teacher just called me and told me she needs to go to the ER, but I had to tell her to call Donna or Charlie." I pressed my lips together, sitting back down, placing my phone back on the table, clicking the green home button to see if Donna or Charlie had responded.

"Is she gonna be okay?" Chris asked.

"The lady said she would." I glanced at Chris. "Barb called me."

Chris nodded. His kids went to the same preschool as Kaleigha.

"She said there was a lot of blood." I couldn't shake the thought of her wanting me and me not being there, just like I hadn't been there when Cara was dying. I felt sick to my stomach. The smell of food made me even more anxious. How was I supposed to eat when my kid was going to the ER?

"Yikes," Keaton said.

"At least she didn't strangle herself," I mumbled. Those blinds scared me. When we moved to our house, I had made sure to buy nothing that could strangle my kiddos. I took in a deep breath, praying, *Please make her okay and protect her and don't let her die, or have an ugly scar, or have a concussion.*

When our food came, Donna called me, so I started to walk out again. "Hey," I said.

"Hey, I'm on my way to pick up Kaleigha now."

"Okay. Thank you so much."

"I'll keep you updated."

"Thank you, Donna."

"Yup. I'll call you when we know more."

"Please let me know how she's doing."

"I will, sweetie."

I knew Kaleigha was probably fine, but I didn't know for sure, and I didn't want to be away from her if something was wrong, like when Cara had died. I prayed, and when I came back in, they asked for an update. I forced myself to eat a few pieces of my burger, taking in the black-and-white tiled floor along with the red booths, chairs, and stools. That's what my therapist had encouraged me to do whenever I'd get anxious, because evidently, a few weeks prior,

I had a panic attack on stage, hence the fact I couldn't breathe or eat. It was happening now, too. I could barely swallow, and I debated whether to try.

"You're not eating much," Chris noticed quietly.

"I'm stressed," I told him honestly.

Next to me, Keaton put a hand on my back. "I would be, too." There was empathy in his voice.

I wanted to leave the table and go sit outside to be alone, but I didn't. As I forced myself to slowly nibble on my hamburger, everything slid out of the bun. I gave up after eating only a third of the burger, because everyone else was finishing up. Donna texted me that she'd gotten Kaleigha to the ER, letting me know she was in good spirits.

We walked back to the church together to get ready for sound check. Our ear monitors were not connecting to the sound system, so we had to troubleshoot. They would not connect no matter what Nate or George tried. They tried restarting them. Nothing. We tried praying. Still nothing. I looked at Keaton.

"You're gonna have to be loud, and everything's on you, dude."

Keaton swore, running a hand down his face. "You're going to want Tennyson back, aren't you?"

Tennyson was better, sure, but only because he'd done it longer.

"It's gonna be fine." I patted him on the back, and he sighed.

"I'll use a metronome still."

"Great."

"We could do an acoustic show," he suggested.

George walked over to us. "We're going to keep trying because it's not working for Hannah and Valerie either."

"Well, shoot." Keaton said.

"No, *trouble*shoot," I said dryly.

Glaring at me, he pretended to be annoyed. "I might quit the band over bad dad jokes," Keaton threatened.

"I might quit the band over your lack of humor."

"At least then your kids could be exposed to more of your dad jokes."

That probably shouldn't have burned as I swallowed. "Sure." I pulled out my phone to see Donna had texted me.

She said they were still waiting, and she sent me a photo of Kaleigha staring at the camera, holding a rag over her forehead as her bottom lip hung out. I couldn't tell for sure, but it looked like her eyes glistened with tears. The only blood I saw was drying on her pink and green shirt Donna had picked out for her because Donna was Super Nana. I had given her money to buy Kaleigha and Bella clothes because I had no idea what they needed or what was stylish.

I showed Keaton and George.

"Aw," George said. "Poor kid."

"Yikes," was all Keaton said.

"She doesn't look too happy," George said quietly. I looked at the photo again, wishing I could hold her.

"I wonder why." Then I looked at George. "Anyway, what do you think is wrong with the ear monitors?"

"It's a connection issue."

"So what should we do?"

"I don't know. Pray," he told me. "Or figure out why it's happening."

Sighing, I ran a hand through my greasy hair. The other thing I hated most about touring was the shower-to-sweating ratio.

"I guess we'll let you know when we figure it out," George said to me.

Groaning, I bit my lip, suddenly even more stressed—doing a show without ear monitors would be a recipe for disaster. I would have to listen very closely to stay on top of the beat. The other guys would have it even worse because they would have to follow me. We had done shows before where the ear monitors failed halfway through, and those were brutal.

28

SAM

"You going to play with us?" I asked Austin as he laid on the couch in the youth room of the church. We'd finally fixed the connection issue.

"Nah, I'm good." He had his eyes glued on his phone.

"Dude, you love carpet ball."

"I've played it enough times."

"Austin," I whined, leaning on the doorframe. "Come on, let's go."

"I'm tired and kind of just wanna be alone."

"Okay." I didn't move.

"Sorry." He glanced up at me.

"Are you okay?"

"Um, honestly, it's been a rough day."

"Why?" I knew Kaleigha had gotten stitches, but maybe there was more to it.

"I . . ." He sighed. "I just . . ." He placed his phone down on his chest. "I don't know." He sounded frustrated.

"You just what?"

"I just . . ." He looked very comfortable wearing gray joggers and a white GreenButton sweatshirt. "I feel bad I'm not home."

"Because of Kaleigha?" I stuffed my hands in the pockets of my sweatpants, gripping my phone.

"Yeah." His voice caught.

"I'm sure she'll be okay," I said. "She's with Cara's mom, so she's in good hands."

"Yeah." He stared into the distance, and his eyes grew misty. After a while, he sat up, planting his feet on the floor.

"Hey," I said quietly, not sure what I was about to say, finding myself walking toward him. "It's okay."

Revealing his faded green earring, his shaggy hair fell over his face as he gripped his forehead. "I just—I should be home right now."

I didn't really know what to say to that.

"Let's go, guys." Chris's excited voice made me jump, booming from down the hallway of this quiet church basement.

"Oh my gosh!" Putting my hand on my heart, I looked at Austin.

"Did I scare you?" Chris asked, stepping in and leaning on the doorframe.

"Yes," I exclaimed.

Austin just looked at him, not smiling.

"Hey," Chris said quietly, walking toward us. "What's up?"

I gazed at Austin, not wanting to speak for him.

"I just wanna go home," Austin confessed.

Chris nodded, sitting on the other side of him. "Mhmm. Why's that?" he asked.

"I wanna be with my kids."

Chris took a moment. "I know it's hard being away from them."

Austin scratched the dark stubble on his face.

"But, hey, you wanna play carpet ball?" Chris asked.

Austin shook his head.

"Come on," I patted his back. "It'll get your mind off things."

"Why don't you wanna play?" Chris asked.

"I just wanna chill," Austin said tiredly.

"Austin," I told him, "part of the reason you travel the country is to find carpet ball tables in church basements."

"The only reason." There was a dryness in his sarcasm.

"Hey." Chris paused. "Are you okay?"

"Um . . ." Austin inhaled slowly. "No."

"You wanna talk about it?" Chris asked.

"Not really." Austin's eyes welled up.

"Man, what's wrong?" Chris pressed.

"I just . . ." Austin shook his head. "I feel like I'm not there for my kids."

"When you're away, it can feel like that," Chris said. "But that doesn't make it true."

"I know, but if I was home, then . . ." Austin trailed off.

"Then what?" I asked.

Austin scoffed, "You'd think I'd learn."

"What do you mean?" Chris asked him.

"Cara died because I was away, and here I am, still doing this."

A lump in my throat that had gone unnoticed fell into my stomach. I couldn't look at him.

Chris bit his upper lip. "What?"

"If I would've been home, she might still be here, because I could've gotten her to the hospital," Austin stated.

"Austin," I said, "Look at me." He did. "Do you blame yourself?"

Staring at the bright orange wall across from him, he said, "I can't change it, and I know that."

"You didn't answer the question," Chris told him.

"It's complicated."

"Austin." I grabbed his forearm. "I know what it's like to blame yourself. And it's not fun." My words cracked.

"She'd probably still be alive if I was home, and I still do the thing that killed her." His words flew out like a machine gun.

"A disease she got on the mission trip killed her, Austin," Chris said.

"Yeah, but if I'd been home, we would have figured out she needed to get to the hospital."

"You really believe that?" Chris asked him quietly.

"I mean, yeah, it's true."

"Austin—" Chris started.

"Hey," I cut Chris off. "I know what it's like to blame yourself for the death of family members, and it's not fun, okay?" My voice cracked.

"It wasn't your fault, Sam," Austin told me without even skipping a beat, now putting a hand on my shoulder.

"I know," I told him, "and Cara's death isn't your fault either."

"Maybe, but that doesn't change the fact I'll always wonder if things could've been different." He looked down. "Sorry to bring this up."

Swallowing hard, I wiped my running nose with my index finger. "No, dude, you can't go down the path I went down. I legitimately thought about suicide, because I couldn't—I got to the point where I wasn't sure I wanted to live with that guilt."

"I'm glad you're here." Austin wrapped an arm around me for a second.

"Yeah, me too." I swallowed back tears. "It's a really dark place to be in, and I don't want that for you."

"What got you through it?" he asked quietly.

Remembering how close I was to attempting suicide, ashamed I hadn't even told my best friends what I was going through, I blinked back tears, telling myself I could break down when this conversation ended. "I don't know, honestly. Counseling. Time? The grace of God. Knowing that it wasn't fair to y'all, or Ali, or anyone."

"When was this?" Austin asked.

"When I was nineteen."

Austin teared up. "Oh my gosh." His voice was shaking. "I would've been so devastated." He buried his eyes in his hands. "I didn't even know." He looked back at me. "I'm sorry." He cleared his throat. "I knew you struggled, but I had no idea that . . ."

"Notice how you're reacting to Sam right now, Austin," Chris said quietly. "And then notice how you're talking to yourself."

Pulling his lips into his mouth, Austin rested his elbows on his knees, looking back at me. "I know it's not my fault," he whispered as a tear slipped from his eye. "But I don't know how to let myself—I don't know how to live with the unknown." He buried his face in his hands again.

"Honestly, there's not a whole lot I can say that will convince you it's not your fault," I said quietly, wiping the moisture from my eyelashes and sniffling. "And maybe you have to lean into the fact you don't know if things could be different. It's in the brokenness that God's grace shines through. His grace is bigger than the biggest war in your heart. His grace is also bigger than your lack of ability to see this getting better."

"If I'm honest, it's really hard to see things getting better right now."

"What do you think won't get better?" Chris asked him.

"Not knowing if my kids could have a mother right now. At least if I'd been home, I'd know."

"If you had been home, and she died," I told him, "you still would've found a way to blame yourself."

Austin played with the finger that should've had a wedding ring. "You're right, which honestly would've been worse." He paused. "But maybe she'd still be here. I know I can't know, but it's . . ." Austin groaned. "I just wish I knew."

"What would knowing give you?" I asked him.

"Permission to grieve." I wondered if he'd meant to say that out loud.

Chris took a deep breath. "You don't feel like you have permission to grieve?"

"Not if she died because of my selfishness."

"Oh, buddy." Chris shifted his body to turn to him. "You being on tour isn't selfish."

"If someone told you that she would have died whether you had been home or not, would you have convinced yourself that it had been your fault she'd gone on the mission trip in the first place?" I asked.

Austin looked up at me, "I already think I should've stopped her from that, too."

"It sounds like you don't like yourself," Chris stated.

Austin didn't say anything.

"And that probably affects the way you think God views you," Chris added. "It probably affects the way you think your daughters view you—the way you think everyone views you."

Austin's jaw tensed up as he nodded. "I mean, I am pretty selfish for still touring."

"I don't—I'm sorry, help me understand why you think that." Chris was genuine.

"Because I . . . I love my job, and my job literally involves people showing up because they like us, and it's—I like the attention. I like being known. I like touring the country and having people want to talk to me. I do it for Jesus, but . . . I should be home with my kids, but I'd rather be on tour than not."

"So you're selfish because you're an extrovert?" Chris raised his eyebrows at him.

"No, I'm doing this for the wrong reasons. I'm not only doing it for God; I'm doing it for myself, too."

"God created you to like music and to like people. That's why you connect with them," Chris told him. "You're not selfish for liking your job. You love talking to people. That's why you're so good at your job. The fact you're even concerned you're being selfish suggests you're not." Chris cleared his throat. "And the fact that Kaleigha wanted you today is a pretty good indication that you're a pretty damn good father. You've been through it, and somehow you still manage to keep going, keep them alive, and keep them happy under the hardest circumstances." Chris was almost yelling with passion, but then he softened his voice. "And you are absolutely allowed to grieve. Everyone knows how much you love Cara. You're not at fault, and you don't have to suppress it anymore. She never thought of you as selfish."

Despite what Chris said, I could tell Austin was still trying to fight back tears. His lip trembled as he covered his face with the sleeves of his white sweatshirt. With an arm around his warm back, I could feel his silent sobs.

When his tears slowed down, he said, "Thank you, guys."

"Are you okay?" I asked him.

"I think so." Then he looked at me. "I really am thankful you're here." He wrapped an arm around my shoulders. "I mean that."

"Thank you." I cleared my throat. "I'm glad you're here, too."

Then he looked at Chris, not wanting to exclude him. "And you, too."

The red in Chris's face matched his bloodshot eyes. "I love you guys so much, and I don't want you guys to ever feel less than."

Austin nodded, wiping his eyes on his sweatshirt sleeve and sniffling loudly. "Thank you." He sighed. "Okay, um, let's go play carpet ball." He looked at me. "Do I look okay?"

"Do you want me to answer honestly?" I smirked.

29

AUSTIN

I was in an oddly upbeat mood—maybe because I was killing Riley in carpet ball—but I also felt like I could burst into tears at the same time. Riley had no idea what had happened on the other side of the basement.

"Dear Lord . . ." I threw the cue ball at the tiebreaker ball, knocking it into the pit. Riley groaned as I put my hands up, whispering, "Yes!"

"It's not over yet," Riley reminded me, slamming two balls on the table for the second tiebreaker.

I picked the darker balls because when I was at camp in 2001, a fellow thirteen-year-old had told me the darker balls were heavier, and therefore it was fact, even all these years later.

Riley threw the cue ball, hitting my dark blue ball into the pit.

"No," I said quietly in mock distress, catching the cue ball, staring down at his two tiebreaker balls, remembering that twenty minutes ago I was literally weeping. I let go of the ball, looking at Chris and Sam playing at the other table. They weren't loud people in general, but right now they were literally silent. I didn't see the cue hit Riley's ball into the pit until Riley groaned.

Strategically, Riley tried to toss the ball down the table, but he missed. Picking the cue ball up, I sighed. "Dear God," I said genuinely, and it was one of those tosses that I just knew would hit it in. "Yes." My voice was still quiet, almost hoarse.

Cursing, Riley started setting up again.

"I'm going to go chill before the Q&A."

"One more game?" Riley pleaded, glancing down at the triangle of six balls he'd already set up.

"Okay, one more game."

30

AUSTIN

"So, if you didn't know, we're GreenButton," I said after our opener. "I know some of you were dragged here, and if that's you, shame on the person who brought you because we're not that good." People chuckled. "Hey, come on, Arizona, you're not supposed to laugh at that." Sighing, I smirked back at Chris who rolled his eyes. "Okay, I mean, at least give us a chance. If you don't like the show, or if you fall asleep, you can email our management." Glancing backstage, I said, "Sorry, Nate, you're gonna be busy for the next few days."

I clipped the capo on my guitar. "By the way, can we give a shout out to our crew? Because they're literally the only reason we're able to do what we do. So, shout out to Nate, our manager, and his wife, Hazel, who runs merch. Go say hi to her after the show. George takes care of sound, so if we start sounding bad, that's totally his fault. Jimmy, our bus driver, is also the best; he gets us from Point Zero to Point A, to Point B, to Point C, and back to Point Zero. Can we give them all a round of applause?" I clapped my hands, and the crowd clapped, too, although they did seem kind of bored.

"So, up here, we have Sam Lowe on keys. This guy is only twenty-one years old, and we kidnapped him when he was seventeen. He has an August birthday. It's fine. We have Chris Thompson to my right—your left—as well. On your right, we have Riley Thompson. No, they're not married; they're brothers. Last but not least, our drummer boy is Keaton Harrington. He's the most qualified person up here, because he just graduated with an MDiv."

I looked back at the audience in the dark. "And I'm Austin Brooklyn. We're from Ames, Iowa, home of Iowa State University." Every time I said this, I felt like I was lying because Sam wasn't actually from Iowa. When a few people cheered, I said, "Hey, like five people know Iowa is even a state! Go Cyclones, even though I went to UNI, but that's beside the point."

We continued on with the show, telling the same stories I'd told over the last few months and some I'd told for the past few years.

But when I pinched the fourth fret with the capo for 'Let Me Trust You,' I decided to announce it was the one-year anniversary, because it almost seemed dishonest not to. I glanced back at Sam as I started picking a random chord, not sure what I would even say. "So, I have a confession," I stated. "I really don't like this next song, and the only reason why we do it is because it's our most popular song." Putting my hands on the body of the guitar, no longer picking for a moment, I added, "I know 'Let Me Trust You' is the reason a lot of you even know who we are, so I'm really sorry if I just broke your heart by admitting that.

"I'm going to get real for a second though, so bear with me." As Sam started improvising on piano to fill in some music, I regretted starting this one-sided conversation with a few thousand people. "A year ago today, we were in Hartford, Connecticut, and it started off like any other day on tour. We woke up late on the bus. We went out to lunch at a local restaurant. We hung out at a coffee shop, even though I don't like coffee that much—the rest of the band does—and then we went back to the church to do a sound check . . . and then I tried to call my wife."

I had told my counselor what had happened, but he was the only person I'd relived it with. "She didn't answer. When we'd left late a few nights before, she had cold-like symptoms, and we didn't think much of it. The last time we'd spoken over the phone, the day before, she hadn't been feeling super well. I encouraged her to go to the doctor, but she said she didn't want to spend the money because we don't have the best health insurance."

I didn't want to talk about this in depth. "Long story short: she was on a mission trip a few weeks before, and we didn't realize she was actually really, really ill. She ended up passing away that afternoon, and . . ."

Why did I think it was a good idea to bring this up? Of course it was tough to talk about. After my conversation with Chris and Sam, I'd told my therapist about that day in the church basement. Then I'd told my therapist about how Cara had died, and I'd choked up then, too. I'd convinced myself that Cara's death had been my fault until I'd processed it out loud to Chris and Sam. The therapist had encouraged me to try to be more open with the people around me, reminding me that Cara's story and even my story reflected God's grace.

I gave the audience a smile, taking a second to find words. "Sorry, I don't talk about this too often, especially not on stage, because I don't want to be that guy who just whines about his sob story." My voice was high. Gross. I took in a deep breath. I had to keep going. "Anyway, the reason why I hate singing the song 'Let Me Trust You' is because it's a prayer that's really scary to pray, right? Trusting God means giving up control, or being okay with not having control of everything—most things."

Then I told the story behind "Let Me Trust You" for the first time since the awards show.

"I've been singing this song every night for the last six months—after we took a six-month break because of everything— and it was made possible by people who donated to a GoFundMe so we could take time to be with our families. If I'm completely honest, I've tried to not focus on the words of this song, to just go through the motions and get through it. And it's ironic because over the past few months, I've never been more anxious, and I've never been more doubtful. There have been nights—we're getting real honest here—but there have been nights I didn't know if I believed anything I was singing or saying.

"That, my friends, was a dark place to be in, and I literally didn't know how much longer I'd be able to tour. Tonight, I'm not up here with the answers, because I still have a million questions, but I'm up here with the humble realization that I am not God, and I don't know everything. What I do know though is that Jesus, the Son of the Creator of everything, died on a cross because He loved us so much and couldn't bear the idea of not being with His precious creations forever. But the story doesn't end there. Jesus came back and conquered death. There's no grave of

His you can visit because death is conquered. A mustard seed of faith is all you need. Because of the cross, there is hope. You don't get all of the answers right now, but God is faithful. I will see Cara again."

That was when my voice broke, because I believed it again. I cleared my throat. "And there is grace for you, no matter what. Even when you think you don't have the strength to trust God, He still is bigger than your lack of strength. He is bigger than any guilt or shame you hold against yourself. He's bigger than your lack of ability to forgive and show yourself grace. He's bigger than your lack of ability to see into the brighter days of the future. He won't let you go. He didn't create you to give up. You will be okay, even if you're not right now. There is hope, and if my wife could have a dying wish, I know it would be that everyone knew that."

I was choking up to the point of no return, so I started playing the opening measures. "No matter where you're at tonight, let's pray this song together."

I barely got through it. I had to fade out some lines because I knew God would let me trust Him, and believing that again, after everything, was overwhelming.

As we got off the stage, Chris said quietly, "I don't even know whether I need to ask if you're okay after that."

"What do you mean?"

"You are okay, aren't you?" His question sounded light. Felt light.

"I am okay." Letting my eyes well up, I admitted, "But it still aches."

He pulled me into an embrace, and I let tears fall down.

"Do you want to talk?"

"I think I did enough of that." I squeezed my nose with the tips of my finger and thumb.

"That was really raw, but really beautiful."

Nodding, I just looked at him through the tears. They weren't tears of deep, dark hopelessness. They were simple tears of grief; I missed her.

31

AUSTIN

"No!" Kaleigha screamed, grabbing onto my leg as I started walking out. "No leaving! I hate you! I hate you!"

"Shhh," I whispered, untangling her arms from my legs. Kneeling, I pulled her into an embrace. She still tried hitting me, and I didn't even condemn it.

"I hate you!" she screamed.

"Then why do you want me to stay?" Two could play at that game. I picked her up, carrying her over to her bed. Her wavy hair, still wet, smelled like lavender.

"'Cause I like you," she told me. Now, I really didn't want to leave. You could like and hate someone at the same time, but she didn't understand the weight of the words she had used, and I didn't know if it was a battle I wanted to fight right now.

"Well, I like you, too." There was amusement in my voice, despite the pain in my chest.

"Why do you go?" she cried into my shoulder.

"Because . . ." Setting her back in her bed, I looked into her eyes. Light leaked in from the hallway. "I have to go to work to make money so we can have this house, so you can eat food, have clothes, have toys . . ." As I said the words out loud, I wondered if I really had to be gone this much. I couldn't do this forever. Even when Cara was still here, this lifestyle was hard to maintain.

"I wanna mommy." She sounded defeated.

Sighing, I still didn't know what to say. *Do not tear up.* I almost said, "You have Nana." But I was glad I didn't, because that wasn't the same. She had been talking about "a mommy" a lot lately. There was a part of me that wanted to say, *You don't need one.* She didn't, actually. Having Donna so present in her life, especially as a strong Christian woman, was a blessing. There were so many good examples in her life who could mentor her to be the girl she was meant to be. I was so thankful for that.

"I know," I whispered.

"Don't go, Daddy."

"I'm sorry," I whispered.

"Mommy's gone." She had pressed recently about not having a mommy, but not like this. Or maybe I was just feeling it for the first time.

"Kaleigha, I'll be back," I told her.

"Mommy's not. I wanna mommy."

"Why?"

"Because mommies are home."

Ouch.

Then she added, "Why is my mommy in Heaven?"

Deep questions a child should never have to ask themselves. I didn't want to cry in front of her. Not because it was shameful, but because I didn't want to scare her. Swallowing back tears, I still didn't know how to explain.

"Remember, she stopped breathing because she was really sick, and when you're not breathing, your body stops working."

"Why was she sick?"

I didn't know how to explain she got a disease while serving God that made her sick enough to die. I didn't want to turn Kaleigha away from serving Jesus. Was I supposed to tell her that her mom was an incredible human? That she would do anything to tell people about Jesus, even if it meant risking her life by going to a country with sickness?

"She . . ." My voice was scratchy, so I took a second to regain strength. "Your mommy was helping people in another country far away where they don't have medicine as good as we do in the United States, and she got sick there, but we didn't know she was sick because sickness takes a while to show sometimes."

"Am I sick?"

"No, no. It wasn't contagious."

"Will I die?"

"Someday. Everyone dies." Why was I having this conversation with my kid?

"Will you die?"

"Someday. But don't worry about it. When you die, you're with God."

"Like Mommy?"

"Yup."

"I wanna be with Mommy," she told me. I heard the tears in her voice.

Me too. But I also wanted to be here.

"Kaleigha." I took a second. She perked up to look at me quickly, her innocent eyes adorable. Her alertness alarmed me—this kid needed to sleep. "Mommy is always with you, even when you can't see her."

"Like God?" she asked quietly.

"Well, sort of. She loves you, and God loves you. She wants you to be nice. God does, too." Cara always treated everyone with kindness, even when they didn't deserve it, including me.

"Okay," she said quietly. "But please don't go," she pleaded with me.

"I wish I could stay."

If I had a typical nine-to-five job, then I wouldn't get to spend the extended chunks of time with Kaleigha and Bella I did get. But it wasn't right that Donna and Charlie were taking care of my kids. It wasn't their job, and maybe the only reason they cut me slack was because of Kelly; they understood that to make an income as a Christian artist, shows were a requirement. Also, Charlie had been deployed three times when Cara was growing up. "But you, my girl, need to go to sleep now." I grabbed her rainbow-maned white stuffed unicorn, Cloudy, making a kissing sound as I bopped her forehead with the unicorn's mouth. "Be a good example for Cloudy and Bella." I threw the covers over her and then kissed her forehead. "And go to sleep." I smoothed her damp hair.

"Don't go," she yelled. "I'll be good."

"You'll be good either way," I told her calmly. "For me, and for Nana and Papa."

"I wanna mommy," she cried out loud, and I cringed at the realization that Donna and Charlie could hear every word. "What if you don't come back?"

We had learned the hard way there were no guarantees, but I took my chances by whispering, "I will. I promise. I'll see you Monday. I love you."

I shut her door behind me, and that was when Donna came up the stairs. I showed her a smile.

"Are you okay?" she asked.

Not knowing what she'd heard, I debated how honest I wanted to be. Glancing down her way, my eyes welled up as I gritted my teeth. I surprised myself by shaking my head. She started toward me, opening her arms. If she had been my own mother, I would've walked into my room, shutting the door in her face. But for some reason, I let Donna embrace me for a second. I pulled away before I lost it.

"I'm gonna finish packing," I told her.

Nodding, she let me go, and I shut my door behind me, almost locking it. I walked over to the two chairs in the nook, more for decoration than use as they were below my TV. They'd been in our old bedroom. This bedroom was designed for two people, not one.

My counselor had encouraged me to not suppress tears, especially if I was alone. I wasn't ready to cry in front of Kaleigha or Bella, though. Not fighting it made me uncomfortable, so I leaned back in the chair, pulling my phone out of my pocket to distract myself, but I didn't have the motivation to type in the passcode. What was I going to do? Scroll and look at other people's lives to make myself feel worse? It sure wouldn't make anything better, so I sat the phone down on the armrest, staring at the green button against the black screen.

It didn't surprise me to hear a knock on my door. I wiped my cheeks with the cuff of my white sweatshirt. "Yeah?" I tried to be polite, even when being intruded on in my own bedroom.

Donna walked in, shutting the door behind her. She sat on the chair opposite of me, which no one else had ever used in this room. I didn't look at her.

"What are you thinking about?" she asked me bluntly.

"I don't want to leave them." I actually meant it.

She reached over, patting my knee. "I know you don't."

We glanced at each other, wondering if we were going to break the unspoken rule of not addressing the impact losing Cara had on us.

"What can I do?" she asked me quietly.

Unable to look at her, I hated that she was seeing me cry as I felt tears run down my cheeks. Why now? Covering my face with my hand, I looked toward the rarely made bed, shaking my head, not knowing how to respond to her question. She was already doing so much for me by watching my kids days on end.

"Austin, talk to me," she pleaded, probably uncomfortable because I hadn't cried in front of her before.

Wiping my cheeks with the palms of my hands, I said honestly, "I don't even know what to say."

"I heard what Kaleigha said," she whispered.

So, she knew I was failing as a parent. It was as bad as it sounded. Embarrassing. "Yeah, I know I can't do this forever," I confessed.

"Do what?"

"Tour."

"What does that mean?"

"I want to be home. Every night."

"When do you wanna stop touring?"

"I don't know," I groaned.

She bit her lip. "Okay. What's leading you to think it might be time?"

"That conversation just now. The stitches and me not being there. My kids not having a mother . . ." My voice faded lower. "Being gone was hard enough with Cara here, but now it's just . . . I don't think I'm supposed to sacrifice the time with my family for something that can easily just be a hobby."

"That's fair. But how are you doing with it?" she asked me.

"Doing with what?"

"Cara's passing."

Please don't do this, Donna. "I'm . . ." Knowing that I had to choose my words wisely in order to be honest, I reminded myself I was not expected to be *good*, whatever that word even meant. "It's just hard."

"What's hard?"

"Everything." My voice wavered. "Literally everything." I took in a deep breath, shaking my head, glancing at the time.

"What does that mean?" Her compassionate mom voice came out, but it was not her job to comfort me.

Massaging my face, I stared at the green button on my phone. "I . . ." I cleared my throat, trying to relax a bit more. *You're fine.* "There's the tension between wanting to tour—because it allows me to do what I love—and the cost that comes with it. My kids need me more than most kids need their dad." Putting a hand up, I added, "I appreciate you and Charlie staying with them, but my kids shouldn't be raised by you guys half the time. Being gone was something I wrestled with before Cara died, too."

Donna grabbed my hand as I bit the inside of my lip.

"What do you think Cara would tell you right now?" Her voice was soft and gentle.

Her hands felt warm around mine. Part of me wished my mom was more like Donna. But at least I had a mom. Kaleigha and Bella would only know their mom through stories and photos.

Imagining Cara with me this upset was a devastating image. We had been married for almost four years; she hadn't seen me cry once. To be fair, there hadn't been any reason to. Not that our marriage was perfect. Leaving every week wasn't easy. We fought sometimes, sure, but life was good. So good. She had been so supportive of my career, even through the sacrifices she had to make. Knowing that Kaleigha and Bella were in very steady, loving hands was the only thing that made being on the road manageable.

If Cara had seen me this upset, I didn't know if she would've known what to do. What to say. In the lowest moments over the last year, I had repressed what it would be like for her to sit with me if it wasn't her who'd died, but another loved one. The idea of her holding me—it was too much to handle.

Donna rubbed my arm before squeezing my shoulder. "What are you thinking about, kiddo?" She held back her own tears, and emotion rang through her voice.

"I don't even know why I'm like this." It wasn't like any of this was new. We had been at this for about a year, but only recently had I been crying about everything.

I caught myself trying to fight back the tears. I stopped. And I considered why I'd fought nearly every instance of crying. Maybe it was because I knew if I did let go, I would lose control of the moment. After a year of uncertainty, I figured my reactions were the one thing I could control. I'd thought if I kept the stiff upper lip, people would see me as resilient, unaffected, and okay. As strong. But I'd loved Cara deeply, which meant losing her cut even deeper. Perhaps real strength equated to experiencing the pain instead of trying to numb it.

"I can guess a reason or two," she mumbled, patting my shoulder.

Giving her an eye roll through a smirk, I said, "Well . . ."

"This is hard for you." She sighed. "And you can sit here and try to appear all calm, cool, and collected, but I know you're hurting. And it's fine if you don't wanna talk, but I want you to know we love you, and even if you feel alone, we're here for you."

"I love you, too." My voice was barely above a whisper. "Like, more than you know. I'm so grateful for you and Charlie in every way."

She stood up to hug me, so I stood up, too, closing my eyes tightly, but no actual tears escaped. When she pulled out of the embrace, I buried my face in my hands. "Okay, now I gotta pack so I can go shower."

"Yeah, you do. You really need one." She patted my arm, smirking, wiping her face.

"At least you're honest." Rubbing my nose, I chuckled. "Cara would say that," I told her confidently. "Now we know where she got her demeaning attitude."

"She just spoke the truth." Donna wasn't sassy all that often, but when her dry humor did come out, it was unexpected and always made me laugh.

"Wow." Feigning offense, I put a hand on my heart. "Ya know, I think I'm just gonna leave the state for about four days."

"That was actually the goal: to kick you out of your own house."

32

AUSTIN

"Random question: how much longer do you wanna tour?" I asked Chris as we walked on a wet and muddy trail. It had just rained.

He looked over at me. "Touring in general?"

I almost slipped on the trail, cursing loudly.

He caught my elbow. "Whoa!" he exclaimed, stabilizing me. "You good, bro?"

"Yeah! Good catch." I turned to face him, realizing I was holding onto his arm somehow. "It's really slippery out here."

"It is." We started walking again, and he said, "Okay, so touring—you want me to be honest?"

"Yeah."

"I'm ready to be done."

"Me too."

"Really?" he asked.

"I just want to be home with my baby girls."

"Are you just saying that because we're in Wyoming with nothing to do but walk around on a muddy trail, or do you mean that?"

"No, I mean it." I stuffed my hands into my pockets, regretting this walk as I saw the mud on my new shoes.

"What changed your mind?"

"Counseling gave me insight as to why I thought I needed to stay in GreenButton to have meaning."

"Mhmm. How so?"

I ran a hand through my shaggy hair. "Other than the fact I really enjoy it—you know I love writing, creating, and doing shows, and you know I love traveling and talking to people—I think I let the band be a god with a little 'g', and I idolized it because I thought if I wasn't in GreenButton, then I was going to starve.

"When I was little, I didn't have many friends, so when GreenButton really got going, it gave me good friends—good role models. It allowed me to feel heard for the first time. Growing up, it was always about Leo and his basketball, or Luke and his football. For me, I sucked at everything sports-related. I was always chosen last. But the band made me feel cool, because we were able to do shows people actually went to, ya know?

"Not to mention, we were sharing the gospel, which was the one thing that had given me meaning and hope when things were tough in middle school and high school. I wanted everyone to have the hope of the gospel, ya know? I want people to know they're loved by God. When I had those few weeks where I didn't even know if I believed in God, I think I started to reflect why I actually do this, too. It's a job security thing, but I only have one life, and there are other great things I can do. In fact, am I really called to do this thing for the next forty years of my life if it's comfortable? My kids need me. They need me to be with them, and I don't know what the label is gonna do, but even if it means we don't put out another album, I'm ready to be done. To rebuild."

Chris took in a deep breath, nodding. "Okay."

"Okay, what?" I looked at him.

"Okay, I'm proud of you. Okay, I'm with you. Okay, let's talk to the label. Okay, let's start the breakdown process."

"Do you think the label will let us stop touring?"

"Don't know."

"We're supposed to have a record come out this fall," I reminded him.

"I know."

"Honestly, most of the songs I've written feel ingenuine."

"What do you mean?"

"I didn't believe it would get better."

"Well, did it?"

"Absolutely."

"What changed?"

"I don't know," I told him honestly.

He let out a small laugh. "Well, you might wanna figure that out, because I can tell you're better, lighter, and dare I say, happier."

I took in a deep breath, wanting to choose my words wisely. "I realized that being depressed wasn't wrong." Then my eyes started to well up, so I stared into the distance of trees and the gray overcast. "But I don't even know. Maybe I realized I wasn't in control and that it wasn't about me. Maybe time. I don't know, but I'm so thankful to be here, and I'm thankful to be alive. I'm thankful to have had six years with Cara. I'm thankful that I get to see her again. I'm thankful for the opportunity to have been able to follow my dream." I paused. "But I think God might have bigger dreams for me."

Chris wiped his nose, sniffling. It was getting cold. "I don't know if this makes it better or worse, but I . . ." He stopped for a second, because his voice caught as he put a light fist over his mouth. "Um, sorry," he said quietly. "I think you should know that if Cara saw you right now, she'd be so proud of you. She'd be proud of the man you've become from the hardest thing you've ever experienced. She'd be proud of you for pulling through it. She'd be proud of you for choosing your kids. And I know you still have really hard days, but you keep going. And it breaks my heart she can't see how strong your faith has become."

Liquid streaked my cheeks, and it wasn't rain. If this conversation was with anyone else, I don't know if I would've let myself shed tears. I didn't even bother wiping them away, keeping my hands in my pockets due to the cold.

I thought about my earring, but the band didn't have to break up in order to not tour. I was at peace because I knew I was doing the right thing, but I wouldn't have chosen this path. And I never had more appreciation for the gift of life.

"Whatcha thinking about?"

"I survived," I said quietly.

"I'm glad."

"And I'm going to be okay."

"You are."

I buried my face in the collar of my GreenButton crew neck to wipe my face. "I'm going to miss this, though." I sniffled.

"Me too."

33

AUSTIN

When I got back from the road, Kaleigha told me about everything they'd done while I was gone. She had pink mac 'n' cheese while I was gone, which I already knew about because Donna had sent me photos. I asked Donna and Charlie to stick around through lunch so we could chat while Bella slept and Kaleigha watched TV.

"What's wrong?" Donna asked me as we sat at the kitchen table. Kaleigha's eyes were glued on the TV. I had told her we had to talk about bills.

"I love my job, but I love my kids more," I said.

"What are you saying?" Donna asked.

"I need to do other things. I'm trying to live the life I had with Cara, but I can't."

Donna's face fell.

Charlie nodded, taking in my words. "What are you going to do?" he asked me.

"I think I'll move back to Ames and go to Iowa State to become a band director."

"But then we'd miss you too much." Donna's eyes were welling up, so I couldn't look at her. "All your friends are here."

"All my friends are music people," I told her.

"So?"

"So . . ." I stared at the table. "I want to—I need to rebuild a life—I need to build something new instead of trying to pick up the broken pieces of something that can't be rebuilt. I loved Cara, and you know that, but I can't pretend like she's not gone and continue the way it was before."

"When are you thinking about stopping?" Charlie asked.

"Probably before the semester starts in the fall."

"No official last tour?" Donna asked.

I shook my head, glancing back at Kaleigha. I had missed her and Bella so much. I missed Cara, too, but my baby girls were still here on Earth.

"You just want to be done?" she asked.

"No, I just want to be home with my kids."

"You're willing to give up your career to be home every night," Donna stated.

"Yes."

"That's affable," Charlie stated.

"What about the label?" Donna asked

"I don't know. We'll see what we can work out, but I don't want to be away much longer."

"Did the conversation you and Kaleigha had the other night change things for you?" Donna pressed.

"Yeah, but it wasn't just that," I told her. "Cara sacrificed most of her dreams for them, and now it's my turn—but it's not even like I'm sacrificing dreams, because I've already lived them. Now my dream is for my kids to know the love their mother showed them, and that love came straight from Jesus." Now, I was tearing up. "And being present with them matters."

"You think moving again is the best thing for them?" Donna was holding back tears.

"I don't know, but touring's not."

"You're going to move them away from us when they've already lost their mom," Donna processed aloud.

Bella and Kaleigha would have to deal with the grief of leaving their Nana and Papa. They were going to have to deal with more hurt now. I hated myself.

"Donna," Charlie snapped, "we're not their parents."

I looked at Donna. "Yeah, and it's not your job to watch them. It's mine. And I know you treat them like your own, which makes being away a little easier, but long term, this isn't what's best for them. You know that."

Donna nodded slowly, taking my hands in hers, and she admitted, "Taking care of them has been a good distraction."

"I know," I whispered. "But you have to take time to grieve Cara, too."

Her face crumbled as she nodded. There was nothing I could say that would take away her pain. She had lost a child, and she would never be able to refill the hole her heart had expanded for her daughter.

Kaleigha noticed Donna was crying, so she ran in to give her a hug. My heart melted.

* * *

I asked Nate to come over that evening because I knew he was working on putting together a fall tour. It was nice outside, so we sat on the back patio. I told him Chris and I were ready to be done. He didn't need to ask questions. He just said, "Okay, we'll talk to the label and see what we can do." And then he requested that Chris and I tell Riley, Sam, and Keaton.

So we did, and it wasn't a shock to any of them. Keaton hadn't been in it for the long haul anyway. Keaton's dad also wasn't doing well, and Keaton told me he was looking at churches to pastor in central Iowa. Riley was excited because then he would be able to tour with Kelly. They were set to get married in the summer.

But I could tell it was news Sam didn't want to hear. Chris and I were most worried about him, so as everyone was leaving, I said to him, "I'm sorry."

"It's not your fault," he told me. "You should be home with your kids." He gave me a smile. "I'll figure it out. I always do."

34

AUSTIN

Sitting down on the couch next to Nate, I looked at Dillon.

"What's going on?" Dillon asked.

"I want to stop touring." Dillon nodded slowly, folding his arms. He wore a blue button-down shirt with jeans that were just a little too tight for him. He glanced at Nate. "That doesn't surprise me."

"Yeah. Sorry." I put my hands up.

"Are you still prepared to produce an album?"

"What are our options?"

"Well, if you're prepared to put out an album, we probably wouldn't market it as much, but we might be able to help you out in other ways."

I didn't believe him. "We wouldn't have to tour?"

"Not for this record. We just wouldn't invest in anything other than making it, and you would have to earn that money back. Marketing would mostly fall on you guys. We'd have to rewrite the contract."

"What if we can't pay you back?"

"Then you do shows again to make money." He paused. "You could just do fewer."

"We're already doing the most we can, Dillon."

"You could spread it over more time."

"I want to go back to school, so I can't tour anymore."

"For what?"

"I'm gonna be a band director."

"That's kind of lame."

Ignoring his comment, I said, "What if we produced an EP instead?"

"Would you be happy with that, though?" Dillon raised his thick black eyebrows that matched his black hair.

I thought about it. "I mean, or we could do a fundraiser for an album and break the contract, and then we'd have more say about how it's produced."

Dillon looked at me. "Look, we'll produce your next record. It's not your fault you need to be home. We'll work it out."

Glancing back at Nate, I nodded, anxious about terminating my income but ready for this next step. "Okay."

"We'll detail out a more flexible contract, okay? We'll figure it out. You and Grayson Clay can do what you want with it." He looked at me. "We're not out to shatter your dreams, Austin." Though he said it lightly, it didn't feel that way.

And in that moment, I admitted to myself it had been my choice to tour.

"Okay. Thank you." I shook his hand. "One more thing." I handed him a CD with Sam's phone number on it. "Sam Lowe should be your next rising star."

35

AUSTIN

Bella and Kaleigha were asked to be flower girls at Riley and Kelly's wedding. Kaleigha would help lead Bella because Kelly really wanted both of them.

The wedding party took photos.

I stood on Riley's side. Megan was Kelly's matron of honor, and Chris was Riley's best man. It was a big wedding party—five on each side. The groomsmen were all the band members. I was partnered with Nikki, a chick who had short brunette hair, curled only for this occasion. She was married, like the rest of Kelly's party. I checked all their left ring fingers. Photos were rough due to the sweltering heat of that July afternoon. Our maroon tuxedos matched the maroon satin gowns the ladies wore.

The photographer, Kayla, asked me if I wanted a photo of just my family. We hadn't had professional photos taken since before Cara had died. There should've been four of us.

"Sure."

Aware of their dresses, I knelt before picking my daughters up, and Bella started playing with my earring.

"That's my ear." I bent my head so it would be harder for her to grab it. She probably noticed it because I'd gotten my hair cut for the wedding—Donna had dropped a few hints.

But as she pulled the top out, the back of the earring fell to the ground, landing somewhere in the grass. Kneeling immediately, I said to both of them. "Get down." Kaleigha hopped off. Taking the earring out of Bella's hand to prevent her from swallowing it, my eyes watered. I held the earring tightly between my index finger and thumb before I found myself pulling both Kaleigha and Bella into a hug.

God was faithful. He sent this sign—it was time to end the band, and I had no idea what I was going to do with my life.

"Did you lose it?" Kayla asked me, kneeling in her light gray dress pants.

Pulling away from the girls, I stood back up, sliding the earring into the pants pocket of the maroon tux because I didn't know where else to put it. And I was okay with the idea of losing it. "Just the back," I croaked.

"What if you grabbed their hands and started walking away from me?" Kayla suggested, bringing me back to the moment.

"Grab Daddy's hands," I said to my kids, glancing over at Chris, smiling, my heart full with peace and growing pains.

Kayla went on to photograph Chris, Megan, and the twins. I chatted with Sam as I kept one eye on Kaleigha, Bella, and Joshua chasing after each other. As we started back into the church, I grabbed Chris's shoulder and whispered, "Bella pulled out my earring."

Chris looked back at me, raising his eyebrows. "When?"

"Just now. While we were taking pictures."

His eyes were watery as he smiled. "That's crazy." His voice grew quiet as we kept our distance.

"Yeah." My voice cracked.

"How do you feel about that?"

"It's the confirmation I needed, but it's still a tough pill to swallow."

"I get that."

"But it's definitely a sign."

"For sure."

* * *

"Kelly has been my friend for the last seven or so years. I knew of her music, and then when I met Chris, I met Austin, so I met Cara, and eventually I met Kelly. Next thing I knew we were all really good friends, and of course Riley and Kelly became more than friends." Megan looked over at Kelly, and I could tell what was coming next by the way her face crumbled, so I braced myself. "And I know I should not be in this spot today, because it should be Cara."

I couldn't even look at Megan, and I wished I couldn't hear her voice break as I stared down, the tears already building up over my eyes. "She would be so proud of you, Kelly." Megan cleared her throat. "I will never try to replace your sister, but I am so excited to call you my sister now, even though you've always been a sister to me. And I know Cara would be devastated that she's not here in the way any of us had expected, but my hope is that you and Riley love each other the way Cara loved Austin, and the way Austin loved Cara. And I know you both will."

I let my hands be the dam against my smooth face, catching the overflow of cleansing water before it could soak my maroon tux as Chris massaged my back. If Cara had still been here to give a speech about our love for each other, I think I would've cried, too.

Cara had deserved more than me, but I had been so lucky.

Megan said a few more words, but I zoned out as she told the story about how Riley used to text Kelly while we were on tour, and how she had told Chris, "They're going to get married." Everyone knew. I'd even told Cara I thought Riley and Kelly were probably sleeping together. Cara had agreed. She hadn't even liked Riley that much, but she still would've supported Kelly.

Kaleigha and Bella stayed home with a babysitter for the reception, but when I realized I actually had no one to dance with, the loneliness hit me, and even though I danced with cute, single girls, I couldn't shake that they weren't Cara. It didn't feel right at all. But I smiled. I talked to them. I asked them about their lives. One of them was an up-and-coming musician, and I couldn't date a traveling musician. If I hadn't stopped listening to Christian music, I maybe even would've heard of her, because she was evidently on the radio. She was also young.

Dancing with other women seemed like cheating.

Even though I didn't want to, I stayed until Kelly and Riley shoved the cake down each other's throats—what a dumb tradition. Cara and I had laughed about how we should've planned that better, because I'd almost gotten cake on her dress.

After that, I walked over to Donna and Charlie. "I think I'm gonna head out," I told them.

Charlie gave me a sad smile. "Already?" He wrapped an arm around me.

I nodded.

"You've been a trooper," he told me. "I know this hasn't been an easy day for you, kiddo."

My eyes started to well up. Again.

Charlie wrapped his other arm around me, giving me a tight embrace. I almost pushed back, but I didn't. I let him hold me. When I pulled away, Donna kissed my cheek before pulling me into a hug. I let her hug me, too. But I forced myself to hold back the tears because I didn't want Kelly or Riley to look over at me and see me cry.

After I finally said goodbye to everyone, I walked out to my car, and there, I lost it as I drove. I debated whether to go home or not. I didn't know how long it was going to last, the slow but involuntary sobbing. It probably wasn't wise to drive while crying, but I hoped it would ease up by the time I got home.

Ali, in town to visit Sam, was kind enough to babysit. My plan had been to shoo her off with cash, but she asked me, "How was the wedding?"

"It was a wedding." I said shortly. "How were the kids?"

"Good." She sat comfortably on the couch. "Bella is really sweet. Kaleigha's funny."

"That's a good way to describe them." Bella was like Cara. Kaleigha was a lot like me.

"You have really well-behaved kids," she told me.

"I lucked out and take little credit."

"What do you mean?"

"My wife was fantastic with them." My voice was uneven as I sniffed a little. "And when I'm away, my in-laws are fantastic with them too."

"Well, I know you play a big part."

Shrugging, I noticed how cute she looked. Her straight hair fell just below her shoulders, a sandy-blonde color. Her brown eyes looked just like Sam's, but Sam and Ali didn't look much like each other otherwise.

"So, I hear y'all are going to stop touring."

"Yup. But Sam's not. He's gonna go solo."

"That's wild to me," she said.

"What? Watching your little brother become famous?"

"Yeah," she beamed. "I'm so proud of him."

"You should be," I told her.

"What will you do next?" she asked me.

"I still don't know. Maybe go back to school to become a band director, but I just—financially, it would be a lot to swing."

"What do you want to do?"

"I want to do something in ministry but not in Nashville."

"Well, the camp I work at is looking for a program director."

"What camp?"

When she told me the name of it, I exclaimed, "I worked there before."

"You did?"

"Yeah, in 2006. I always wanted to go back, but the band had so many gigs, and it was just too hard to do both."

"You should apply! They really need someone outgoing who loves Jesus."

"Can you send me the details?"

"Sure, I'll talk to my boss, Billie."

"Billie is still there?"

"Yeah!"

Ali gave me her number, promising to talk to Billie about the position when she got back to Iowa. We chatted for a little while about life, but I wore my exhaustion on my face, so she left to go back to Sam's place. I told her to text me when she was back there safely because Sam probably wouldn't be home yet.

Before showering, I pulled the earring out of my pocket, somewhat surprised it was still there. I wondered what I was supposed to do with this piece of green jewelry. After I had lost the first one, I had told Cara I didn't want to lose the other one because I didn't want to accidentally cause the band's demise. She'd told me to push the back closer to the ear. The hole that had hosted the earring was thick and hard. I wondered if the hole would ever close.

I decided to put the earring in the same box with our wedding bands. Looking at her rings with mine made my tears come again. I shut the box, glancing at the garment bag that held her wedding dress.

I needed to shower, so I did. I threw on a white Kelly Minty T-shirt and blue athletic shorts to cool down. I didn't want to be lonely in my bedroom, so I walked down one half-flight of steps and up the other half-flight to go into the studio, landing in front of the piano, challenging myself to write something. But not just anything. I wanted to write something that represented today. Or the last year. Or the last sixteen months. So I grabbed my tablet and I went for it.

This is the sad song I never thought I'd write
And I know you wouldn't try to tell me it's all right
As I lose the fight to hold it all together
Because it hurts me that we're not together
That we won't grow old together
And I wonder if the pain will be in vain
As I wander through the valley of deep, deep waters
I was drowning for a while
I was dying for a while
I'm so proud to be floating
I'm so proud to be surviving
But you'd want me to be swimming
And you'd want me to be thriving
And if you were here right now,
The sorrow would break your heart
Because death did us part
And you had a piece of me,
So losing you tore me apart,
Shattering what was left of me
The old me is gone
I'll never be the same
This is the sad song I never thought I'd write
Because you wouldn't tell me it's all right
As I lose the fight to hold it all together
Because it hurts me that we're not together
That we won't grow old together
And I wonder if the pain will be in vain
As I wander through the valley of deep, deep waters
I tried to fly when I was meant to swim

I tried to forget
I tried to numb it all
I put up walls after I had fallen down
So no one would know
How broken I was
How broken I am
But the walls couldn't withstand the flood
Of blood, sweat, and tears from the fight
To hold it all together
Because it hurts me that we're not together
That we won't grow old together
And you won't see our daughters grow up
This is the sad song I never thought I'd write
Because I thought I was going to drown
I didn't think I'd make it to the other side
But I'm here because of the tears I've cried,
Thankful for the memories we made
And I still cry because you loved me so well
This well will never drain
But pain was not in vain
Because you showed me what love really is
And I will love well because of you
I made it to the other side
To write the sad song I never thought I'd write
But I will love our daughters well
I will love our neighbors well
I will show our daughters how to love well
This well of gratitude can never drain
Because I'm able to write the sad song I never thought I'd write

Lyrics came first, and then the melody I started recording on my phone. Playing around with it quietly on the piano, I wanted to nail down the minor key, a territory we hadn't experimented with a ton. I typically didn't write slow piano ballads. Usually, our producer or Sam would write the piano part, but this was meant to be written by me.

After an hour or so, I recorded a really rough demo, which took a couple of takes because I kept screwing up the accompaniment. I didn't cry while recording, but when I listened to the finished product, I bawled because I knew that it was special. And sad. And pretty. And I survived.

And I missed her.

There was no pressure, because my career was no longer at stake. If the song did well, great. If not, oh well. Life was short. I'd lived my dream. My new dream was to love my kids well. Memories were worth cherishing, but the future was in front of us.

EPILOGUE

AUSTIN

I held Bella on my hip so she could see what was happening as the guy over the store counter set up my new phone. Kaleigha was sitting on a stool, folding her hands, staring up at the guy. I stared at the green button on my old phone. It was the end of a legacy. No more phones with green buttons. I was okay with this; blue was my favorite color anyway.

A slow piano song played in the background. I smiled at the familiar melody. I'd been told "Sad Song" had made it to mainstream radio, but I'd never been able to catch it, because I didn't listen to those kinds of stations. I hadn't heard it since the day we'd officially recorded it, so it had been well over a year.

"Daddy!" Kaleigha said. "It's your song!"

"Yeah! How do you know that?"

"Grandma likes this song."

The dude who was helping us said, "I bet he wrote it, too." His tone told me he didn't believe that I had.

"He sings it!" Kaleigha exclaimed.

"I do—well, I did." This wasn't something that happened very often. I wasn't one to tell people, "Hey, I wrote this song."

"What's the name of the song?" he quizzed.

"'Sad Song'."

"Who's it by?"

"GreenButton."

He looked down at the old phone's green button and then back up at me, his eyes narrowing.

"Oh my God, you actually wrote it?"

"Yeah."

"I heard this song a few months after my mom passed away, and I looked it up, and it . . ." He blinked a couple of times.

"I'm sorry, man."

"Yeah, um, this song cycles through our playlist, so I finally looked it up, and it made me cry, because my mom was the most loving person I'd ever met, and I try to live like she did, and—" He looked at me. "Is there a story behind the song?"

"Yeah. There is." I gave him a smile. I placed a hand on Kaleigha's head and squeezed Bella a little tighter. "Their mom was a missionary, and she passed away after getting sick on a trip. She brought a lot of people hope."

"Oh, wow, I'm so sorry," the dude said.

"You miss Mommy." Bella kissed my cheek.

I'd been more open with Kaleigha and Bella about who their mother was. "Yeah, I do, kiddo."

"I miss Mommy sometimes." Kaleigha leaned her back against my stomach.

"That's hard. My mommy died, too," the dude said to her. "But you have a daddy who loves you very much."

"I know!" Kaleigha said, kissing the sleeve of my Iowa State sweatshirt.

"Thanks for saying something," I told him.

He wiped his eyes. "I think this is a sign."

"Probably. I also haven't listened to the song since it came out, so it's emotional for me, too."

"Wait, really?"

"Yeah, I don't actively listen to our stuff."

"But your song is literally on the radio."

"So I've been told."

"What do you listen to?"

"My kids talk." I smirked down at them. "Or worship music, because I sing at church sometimes."

He chuckled. "Where at?"

I told him the name of the church I belonged to.

"I might have to check it out."

"You definitely should."

"Are you a worship pastor?"

"No. I work at a Bible camp, and I'm in school."

"Nice!" Then he asked, "Can I get a photo with you?"

"Only if we take it on my new phone so I can test out the camera. I'll send it to you."

So, I took a selfie with him and the girls as a text from Ali popped up. She would be coming over for dinner that evening to hang out with the girls and me.

Looking at the photo now, I notice the fullness of life in my girls' eyes and the hope and peace of my smile.

AUTHOR'S NOTE

Dear Reader,

First of all, thank you for taking the time to read *GreenButton*. I hope you enjoyed reading it as much as I enjoyed creating it.

As a twenty-year-old female, I was initially apprehensive about writing from the point-of-view of five older men, three of them fathers. A part of me worried I would be judged as some chick forcing her uneducated stance on toxic masculinity, which has never been my intention. Writing about situations I haven't personally experienced wasn't something I took lightly either. But I've had the desire to publish the story of *GreenButton* ever since I concocted these imperfect characters that I've grown to know and love.

Some of the best advice I've ever heard was something along the lines of, "Creators do the best work when they stop caring about what others think." Keeping that in mind, I did my best to allow each character to experience their story in the most authentic way possible, leaving any fears about criticism behind.

As the writer, I have the responsibility to be authentic, too: I understand what it's like to resist the urge to cry. Though this novel is written from the perspective of five different men, guys are not the only people who experience the desire to push back their emotions. Women do it, too. I don't cry a lot, which may be why I'm tempted to put a guard up when I *do* need to cry. Art is not always a direct reflection of the artist; however, I take ownership of the parts of me that were reflected in my characters throughout this piece. Sometimes beautiful paintings have dark colors.

My hope is that we as people—no matter who we are—learn to accept that we feel things. There are moments where our bodies physically need to let the dam break, and the aftermath of a flood can be messy. With that said, feelings may not always flow out in tears. For me, a lot of the time, my outlet is writing (hence this novel). Another way I process my emotions is by talking things out, whether it's with friends, family, or my therapist. It also looks like accepting my thoughts, fears, and emotions for what they are, and striving to not judge myself for how I feel. All in all, I hope this is permission for you to experience life: foggy stormy nights meeting the rainbow against the sunrise, because the sun always rises.

With grace and peace,
Kayla

ACKNOWLEDGMENTS

Whew, we made it. Writing and publishing this novel has been a wild ride but so worth it. None of this would have been worth it without you, the reader. Thank you for reading my book. Thank you for taking a chance on reading a self-published novel. Thank you for taking a chance on me.

I want to start off by thanking Victoria Harrison, my best friend from school, for helping me develop this story since 2014 when the plotline and the characters first came to mind. We were thirteen. Mo (Imogen) was inspired by a character that was initially conceived by Victoria. We went through an extended phase in 2015 of constantly texting out scenes with the majority of the characters in this novel. Over the last seven years, she's also been there to watch the characters mature along with us. I love you, Victoria.

Stettson Smith, you are one of my best friends here at college. Thank you for talking through various scenes with me over the last year. Our conversations about *GreenButton* encouraged me to actually take initiative and rewrite the novel one more time. Thank you for your friendship.

Thank you to everyone who donated to the Kickstarter campaign. Every single one of you who donated made publishing *GreenButton* possible. Y'all funded the campaign in only nine days. It still blows my mind to know forty-nine of you pledged to the campaign and some of you backed me privately, simply because you believed in my project. What means the most is I know the vast majority of you individually. You made this possible. Thank you. Thank you. Thank you.

My editors, Trevor Hightower and Tim Pietz, were incredible. Thank you, Trevor, for giving me your honest opinions while line editing, and thank you for writing the blurb for the book. Tim, thank you for proofreading the novel. Thank you, Natalie Lang, for designing the cover. To the people who took the time to read the manuscript before publication, thank you for your time and feedback.

Jason Boggess, Sam Hackbart, Julia Howes, Ashley Corryn, and my parents are all people who have contributed to an open dialogue regarding the novel; your support hasn't gone unnoticed. Thank you. I also won't forget my friends and family who have allowed me to sprinkle in conversation about *GreenButton*.

Shout out to coffee shops that have housed me literally every day as I've done everything from brainstorming to the final editing. Iced vanilla lattes have been my fuel through this project. So has the disease of procrastination. As the pile of academic papers and assignments built up, I found myself writing *GreenButton* instead. The caveat is I do my best work when I procrastinate on homework, so shout out to all of my professors. (I think?)

But in all seriousness, I'm thankful for the gift of life that God has given me. I'm thankful to have been given the passion for writing and processing and experiencing.